STORM
MOUNTAIN

STORM MOUNTAIN

TOM BIRDSEYE

To the Heater Family,

Climb on!

2011

Holiday House / New York

Library of Congress Cataloging-in-Publication Data

Birdseye, Tom.
Storm Mountain / by Tom Birdseye. — 1st ed.
p. cm.
Summary: Two thirteen-year-old cousins are trapped in a blizzard on the same
treacherous mountain in the Cascades that claimed the lives of their world-famous,
mountain-climber, twin fathers exactly two years earlier.
ISBN 978-0-8234-2130-5 (hardcover)
[1. Cousins—Fiction. 2. Mountaineering—Fiction. 3. Adventure and adventurers—
Fiction. 4. Blizzards—Fiction. 5. Survival—Fiction. 6. Cascade Range—Fiction.
7. Washington (State)—Fiction.] I. Title.
PZ7.B5213St 2010
[Fic]—dc22
2010005768

To my father,
Irving Birdseye,
who also loved mountains
1920–1974

CONTENTS

CHAPTER 1

KNOCK, KNOCK, WHO'S THERE?

Cat Taylor opened the oven door and pumped a fist in triumph. "Yes!" She grabbed a pot holder from its wooden peg, took a deep breath to steady herself, then carefully hauled a twelve-inch, homemade pizza out into the warm glow of the kitchen.

"Perfecto!" she said, surveying her masterpiece. "Thin crust, pesto sauce, black olives, and artichoke hearts. Who could ask for more?" She tucked a stray strand of dark hair behind her ear and grinned.

Until she spotted her dog, a husky named Mugs, sneaking around the corner. The grin dropped. "Hey, you, keep your distance," Cat warned. "Sit."

Mugs didn't sit. He'd made it clear from day one that following directions was not a high priority, especially when there was food to be had. Cat figured that in another life Mugs must have been a pig—with hollow legs. The rascal could flat-out eat. Now the greedy gleam in his eyes shined clear. He'd scarf down every last bit of her prized pizza in a heartbeat if he got the chance.

"No way," Cat said. She put the baking sheet on the counter. "I agree that this is the best pizza in the world, but Mom made me promise not to feed you human food, remember?"

Cat waited for an answer, then caught herself and thumped her forehead with the palm of her hand. There she went again, talking to Mugs like the dog was human. Ridiculous.

Or was it? Who else was there to talk to at the end of three miles of winding, rutted gravel known as Storm Mountain Road? Trees were plentiful. People were most definitely not.

Of course she texted her friends in town, visited their Facebook pages, and chatted regularly with them on her cell. But it wasn't the same as having a real person in front of her.

True, her mom, Hope, was usually around. A freelance software developer, she telecommuted from her office just down the hall. Hope would instantly drop her work if Cat needed anything. She tried really hard to be Cat's friend, and Cat appreciated the thought. But Hope *wasn't* Cat's friend. She was her mother, and there were some things—no, actually, there were *lots* of things—that Cat didn't want to discuss with her mother.

Besides, Hope wasn't home tonight, anyway. In an uncharacteristic move that had caught Cat completely by surprise, Hope had agreed to give a presentation at a software developers' conference in Portland. In the past she'd always said she'd rather swim with sharks than speak in public, and yet she'd driven all the way to the city to stand up in front of hundreds of strangers.

What was with that? Especially on this particular weekend in May . . .

Oh well, no matter. Bottom line: Mom wouldn't be back until Sunday afternoon, and that left Cat with Mugs. So even if the pooch didn't have a lot to actually say, he had a way of looking Cat right in the eye that at least gave the impression he was listening, and understood.

Now Cat leaned down and tousled Mugs's furry, pointed ears. "It's you and me, boy," she said.

Mugs looked up at the countertop where Cat had set the pizza, and whined.

"Patience, Mugsy," Cat said. "I haven't forgotten your chow. We're just dining late because . . . well, because we can!"

Mugs wagged his tail. Cat nodded and grinned. "Yep, we are completely, totally, absolutely in charge of our own destiny. You can gobble as much dog food as you want, and I'm going to savor this entire pizza. Then I'm going to wash it down with a Cat Taylor double-shot mocha and stay up all night if I want to!"

Mugs cocked his head and seemed to smile.

"Good boy," Cat said. "Now let's shake on it." She extended her free hand. "C'mon, Mugs, shake."

No response, as usual. Despite countless hours of effort on Cat's part, her dog was simply *not* into learning tricks.

Cat sighed. "Mugs," she said, for what felt like the millionth time, "you're hopeless."

Mugs answered with a lunge for the countertop and almost

nabbed the pizza. Cat scooped it up, laughing. "Get back, you rascal!"

Mugs barked and lunged again.

Cat held the pizza over her head and danced around the kitchen, chanting, "No pizza for Mugs! No pizza for Mugs! No pizza for—"

BANG! The knock at the front door boomed so sudden and loud, Cat almost dropped her dinner. "Whoa!"

BANG-BANG-BANG! The pounding echoed through the house. Mugs bayed like a hound on the hunt and dashed into the living room.

Cat shoved the pizza to the back of the counter and followed, although she wasn't sure why. Alarm bells were going off in her head. "Who is it, Mugs?" she whispered. "Who would be way out here in the boonies, especially this late at night?"

She tiptoed over to the front window and peeked around the curtain. A face loomed inches from her own, nose plastered flat against the glass, lips curled in a crazed grin.

CHAPTER 2

A DEER IN THE HEADLIGHTS

Cat gasped and lurched backward, tripping over Mugs. Both girl and dog let out a yelp. Cat crashed to the floor. Mugs squeezed under the coffee table, where he crouched, trembling.

Staggering to her feet, Cat fumbled to get her cell phone out of her pocket. How many times had she rehearsed the proper response to a crisis? Hundreds, surely. But now that the moment was upon her, she had to shout mental directions to herself. Open the phone! Dial nine-one-one! Hurry! A maniac is lurking on the front porch!

BANG! BANG-BANG! "Cat? Hey, is that you? What's going on in there?"

At the sound of her name, Cat stopped and lowered her phone. She tried to calm the hammering in her chest, slow her rapid-fire breathing. Think! she commanded herself. It sounded like a boy. A boy who knew her . . .

BANG-BANG-BANG! "Cat? Sorry. I didn't mean to scare you. I was just fooling around. It's okay, open up."

Now Cat scowled. Scare her? She wasn't scared, just startled, that's all. She shut her phone and slipped it back into her pocket. Scared? Says who? She squared her shoulders, took a deep breath, then undid the lock and eased the door ajar.

It was a boy, all right, standing in the pool of porch light. He wore a frayed red mountaineering parka so large it ballooned around his middle. A backpack was slung over his shoulders. Black hair peeked out from under a neon orange stocking cap. "Hey!" he said, and flashed a broad smile.

Cat stared, unable to believe her eyes.

"What's the matter, *cat* got your tongue?" the boy said. He started to laugh but stopped short. "Get it? *Cat* got your tongue? It's kind of a . . . joke?" He tilted his head. "Um, guess not. Anyway, cool to see ya' again. Sorry about not keeping in touch, but—"

The boy broke off midsentence and waved his hand in front of Cat's face. "Hello? You all right in there? You're looking a lot like a deer in the headlights."

That's because all of a sudden Cat *felt* a lot like a deer in the headlights—blinded in the face of oncoming traffic. Before her stood her cousin Ty. Who, just like her, had lost his father on the North Face of Storm Mountain two years ago. Cousin Ty, who, just like her, could understand what it meant to live with—

"Aunt Hope here?" Ty said. He peered over Cat's shoulder into the house. "She still doing her software thing? Still volunteer with Search and Rescue? How about chicken fajitas? She still make that on Monday nights? She remarry?"

An old, familiar irritation flickered to life in Cat's gut. Although Ty had grown at least a foot and *looked* more mature than the last time she'd seen him, he wasn't. Same old motor-mouth as when he lived down the road. Same old nosy questions, too.

Ty beamed. "Bet Aunt Hope will be glad to see me, huh?"

"She's in Portland," Cat said tersely. "Conference. Home Sunday."

Ty's eyebrows went up. "That's a sign. I mean, what are the odds? My mom's gone for the weekend, too. She and Gene went to her twentieth high school reunion in Spokane and—"

"Stop!" Cat held up her hand like a cop at an intersection. "*Who* is Gene?"

Ty chuckled, clearly delighted to get a rise out of her. "About a year ago Mom went out for a jog and met this runner guy named Gene. One thing, as they say, led to another. She's Lizzy Blake now, not Lizzy Taylor. Gene Blake is my new dad. *Comprendes?*"

Cat shook her head. No, she didn't understand. A new father? How could anyone ever replace—

"Mom thinks I'm bunking with my friend Alex while she and Gene are gone," Ty said. "But I pulled a fast one on her and have been staying home solo."

He hesitated for a moment, as if he expected to be congratu- lated. For what? Pulling a "fast one" on his mom? Maybe on

7

occasion there were a few minor things Cat didn't tell her mother about—staying up all night drinking mochas, for example. And watching teen vampire movies. And, okay, she had to admit Hope knew nothing of her trips to the rock climbing gym in town after school or her vow to follow in Dad's mountaineering footsteps. But that was different. That was to save her mom from worrying.

"Anyway," Ty went on, "I camped out on the couch and played video games, watched Comedy Central, scarfed bean burritos with extra cheese—best food in the world, by the way, especially when washed down with a few cans of Mountain Dew—and just cooled my jets. Well, cooled my jets until early this morning when I woke up right out of a dream."

Ty blinked his eyes shut and then popped them open wide to demonstrate waking up. "I didn't remember much," he said. "You know how dreams are. Dad had been in it, though, I was sure of that. And, okay, I realize this may sound kind of crazy or, you know, sort of *woo-woo,* but it seemed like he had been trying to tell me something. I didn't have a clue what, but I just couldn't get the idea out of my mind."

To emphasize his point, he tapped the side of his head. "So I climbed the ladder into the attic and worked my way back to the corner where Mom had stashed Dad's climbing gear. I started nosing around, and down in the bottom of the last box was his old parka. This is it, right here!"

He turned to the side and did an exaggerated impression of a fashion designer, complete with a fake French accent. "Notice zee fine detailing." He swept his hand down one sleeve. "Especially zee duct-tape patch on zee elbow!"

When Cat didn't respond, Ty shrugged and continued in plain English. "I put it on, pulled the collar up around my neck, and stuck my hands down deep in the pockets. And that's when— *ka-ching!*—I realized what Dad had been trying to tell me."

A sudden sadness swept over Ty's face, and for a tense moment Cat thought he was actually going to cry. What would she do about that? Barricade herself in her room like she did when Mom broke down?

Cat was both relieved and surprised when instead of crying, Ty let out a satisfied sigh. "So I grabbed Dad's search-and-rescue gear," he said, "packed his ashes, and caught the first Amtrak south."

Cat's mouth fell open. Surely she hadn't heard that right. "You packed *what?*"

Ty nodded, smiling now with obvious pride. "Yep, packed Dad's ashes, took Amtrak to Portland, caught Greyhound to town, then hiked the last few miles up Storm Mountain Road. So here I am, and here . . ."

He swung the backpack off his shoulders, and Cat could see that it was a Black Diamond Ascent, same as her dad's. It even had the official Storm Mountain Search and Rescue patch sewn on to the top pouch. Ty opened it and unloaded a coil of red climbing rope and two Petzl ice axes, the kind with curved shafts and aggressive, sharp picks for scaling steep routes. With a grunt, he then pulled out a simple brass urn about twelve inches high.

"Good," he said, looking the urn over. "No scratches. The bubble wrap worked."

He blew a piece of lint off the latched lid, then held it up for Cat to see. "And here's my dad, better known to you as Uncle Scott." He looked into the house again. "Where's Uncle Jonathan? You spread his ashes already?"

Cat's head swam. To steady herself, she put a hand on the back of the stuffed armchair. She glanced over her shoulder toward the little shrine her mother maintained on the living room mantel. In the center of a neat line of wood-framed photos of her father sat a brass urn identical to the one Ty held. "Um, no," she finally mumbled, "Dad's still here."

"Cool," Ty said. He had slipped over the doorsill and now stood beside her. "No, better than cool, it's another sign. It means that you're supposed to join me on—Hey, a dog! Man, I *love* dogs, especially huskies. He's new to the family, huh? When did you get him? What's his name?"

Cat blinked, trying to keep up. Mugs had squirmed out from under the coffee table and was sitting at Ty's feet, looking up at him with his head cocked. "We got him two years ago," she said, "a few days after . . . after you left. His name is Mugs."

Ty crouched and put his hand out. "Hey, Mugs!" he said. "Glad to meet you. Put her there. Shake!"

Cat started to warn him. "He doesn't—"

Mugs shook. Cat couldn't believe it.

Ty rubbed Mugs's ears just the way Mugs liked it. "Great dog. We should take him with us!"

Cat blinked again. "Take him with us?"

But Ty, urn tucked under his arm, was already up and dragging his dad's gear down the hall. "Got to get some sleep first, though," he called back over his shoulder. "Since Aunt Hope isn't home, all right if I crash in her bed?"

He stopped and pointed into Cat's mother's bedroom. "This is it right here, isn't it, across from yours? Yep, same bedspread. Nice and neat, too, just like always." He looked Cat's way. "Don't worry, I won't make a mess. I've turned over a new leaf. I'm organized! Hey, I even brought one of those little travel alarms with me. Gonna set it for five A.M. I'll wake you up, too—promise—so we get this expedition rolling!"

"Expedition?" Cat finally managed to slip in. "*What* are you talking about?"

Ty grinned. "You and me, Cuz, fulfilling the dream. We're going to spread our dads' ashes from the summit of Storm Mountain."

CHAPTER 3

YOU CAN THANK ME LATER

Cat stared in disbelief. "You've got to be kidding."

Ty's grin faded into a thin straight line. "Do I look like I'm kidding?"

Even from down the hall, Cat could see a look of pure determination in his eyes. "But . . . but that's crazy," she said.

Ty flinched at the word *crazy*. "No, it's not." He brushed the air with his hand, as if to dismiss her. "But, hey, if you don't have the guts, I'll do it by myself."

"By yourself? You know nothing about climbing," Cat said.

"And you do?" Ty shot back, sarcasm dripping.

Cat bristled. "Yes, I do!" She advanced on her cousin, finger wagging. "While you were in town all of those Saturdays goofing off on your skateboard, I was learning with Dad. He taught me how to tie lots of knots, and strap on crampons and self arrest with an ice ax, and all sorts of stuff. He even gave me his mountaineering library. Look!"

Cat marched into her bedroom and pointed at the neatly arranged shelves. "Forty—no, *fifty*—books, and I've read them *all*!"

She swept her hand across the spines as she rattled off titles. "*Into Thin Air, Touching the Void, Four Against Everest, No Shortcuts to the Top, Glacier Travel and Crevasse Rescue.* And, of course, *Mountaineering: The Freedom of the Hills.* I've about memorized that one! I could go on and on. Yep, fifty books, easy!"

Ty rolled his eyes. "Woo-hoo, good for you."

Cat ignored the mocking tone. To her, this was serious business.

"And that's not counting all my issues of *Climbing* magazine and *Rock and Ice* and *Alpinist,*" she said. "Or all the Web sites I've bookmarked. I'll bet you haven't read a word of *any* of this stuff, much less studied the topos like I have!" She motioned around the room at the topographic maps that papered the walls. "Storm Mountain is no place for rookies!"

"I'm *not* a rookie," Ty insisted. "I'm the son of Scott Taylor. I can do it. Hey, I'll betcha even Mugs can do it! Right, Mugs?"

Mugs had followed Cat down the hall and jumped up onto the foot of her bed, his usual perch. During the day the spot served as a sentry post from which he could look out the window with quivering anticipation and bark at squirrels raiding the bird feeder. Now, however, he looked back and forth between Cat and Ty, ears perked.

Cat shook her head. "Our dads were expert climbers and look what happened to them up there on the mountain!"

Ty frowned. "I know, I know, but—"

"But nothing!" Cat cut in. "Look at this." She dropped to her knees in front of her filing cabinet, opened the bottom drawer, and pulled out a folder marked DAD. The first clipping, worn from handling and already starting to turn yellow with age, was from the front page of the *Storm Mountain Gazette*. Cat held it up, stabbing her finger at the headline:

Search and Rescue Team
Scott and Jonathan Taylor
Lost on North Face
of Storm Mountain

"Remember, Ty? They knew bad weather was in the forecast, but I guess they figured they could go light and fast and beat it, pull off a save. 'Steal the jewel from under the nose of the dragon,' like they used to say. Every climber was family to them and worth the risk."

"Honoring our dads by spreading their ashes is worth the risk," Ty said.

Cat stood and yanked a short piece of blue climbing rope from her pants pocket. She kept it handy for practicing knots. Pacing back and forth in her room, she automatically looped the rope into her all-time favorite, the first one Dad had taught her—the figure-eight follow-through, used for tying into a climbing harness. Simple and clean, a thing of beauty when done correctly, it was the kind of knot a climber could count on to hold.

"Things can go bad up there in a heartbeat," Cat said. "You're talking about spreading ashes from the summit. Dad and Uncle Scott were only halfway up when the storm roared in. Visibility near zero. Wind gusted over a hundred miles an hour. That's strong enough to rip the goggles from your face, literally tear you off the mountain and rag doll you into space."

Cat tumbled her index fingers in front of Ty's face, one over the other, to demonstrate the force of the wind.

Ty shrugged. "Yeah, I get that."

"That storm raged for nearly a week," Cat said. "Helicopters were grounded, rescuers pushed back. Even though our dads dug a snow cave on a ledge, by the time the weather finally cleared . . . it was too late."

"I know," Ty said. "I *know*."

"Really?" Cat said. She untied the figure-eight follow-through, then quickly tied it again. "Dad and Uncle Scott had climbed all over the world. They were the famous Taylor twins, who'd put up new routes in Alaska, the Andes, the Himalayas, the Karakorams in Pakistan, and rescued dozens right here on Storm Mountain. They'd climb routes most people wouldn't even consider, then ski off the summit just for fun! And they did it all in true alpine style—no bottled oxygen, no sherpas, nothing but what they could carry on their backs. They were pros, and real heroes. Magazines published articles about the famous

Taylor twins. And still they died. Facts don't lie. Storm Mountain is a *killer*!"

Ty raised an eyebrow and faked a horrified expression.

Cat let out a puff of exasperation. She stuffed her practice cord back into her pants pocket. "I've got gear, just like you," she said. "See?"

She moved to the corner of her room, where she stepped into her mountaineer boots, then swept up her father's loaded pack and slung it over her shoulders. With a flourish she snapped the hip and chest straps snug. "Give me ten seconds and I'm ready for anything," she said. "But that doesn't mean I go chasing after disaster!"

Ty glared. "I'm *not* chasing after disaster."

"Yes, you *are*!'"

"No, I'm *not*."

Cat threw up her hands. "Okay, see if I care! Climb!"

"I will!" Ty yelled, and stalked across the hall, slamming Hope's bedroom door behind him.

Mugs let out a soft whine and nudged Cat's hand with his nose. Cat took a deep breath, sighed, and patted him on the head. "Yeah, I know—he's nuts, but we can't let him go kill himself." She looked around her room. "What I've got to do is use all this stuff to put together a reality check that will actually bring him to his senses. I need to be like a lawyer presenting a case in court."

She nodded. "I'll back up my argument with plenty of examples—logical, rational, *real-world* examples, not dreams— and he'll *have* to accept the truth: Stay off Storm Mountain."

Cat cinched the straps of her dad's pack tighter, then started grabbing books off the shelves, magazines from the stacks, more files from the cabinet. Plopping down onto the floor, she spread her ammo out and began thumbing here and there, marking paragraphs to quote and intimidating photos to show— especially the eight-by-ten of dark clouds looming over Storm Mountain.

Speaking of weather, she'd print out the forecast to show Ty too. An unstable air mass was moving in fast, which was not good. Add to that a few grisly climbing disaster stories and she'd really be driving her point home.

Cat woke curled on the floor, sunlight streaming through her window. She sat up, stiff, groggy. The last thing she remembered was Mugs snoring on her bed, doggy head on her pillow, fidgeting as he no doubt chased squirrels in his dreams. The clock had read 3:24 A.M. Now Mugs stood by the bedroom door, prancing. Cat rubbed at the fog in her eyes, then squinted at the radio alarm's digital dial.

In an instant she jolted fully awake. *6:09?* Ty was going to leave at 5:00! She jumped to her feet and staggered sideways under the lurching weight of her dad's pack, barely catching herself on the bedpost. She shook her head. Must have fallen asleep with the pack still on, boots, too. No time to think about that now, though. Gotta collar Ty. She yanked the bedroom door open, to find a note just outside on the hallway floor.

Hey. Sorry about the blowup. Just like old times, huh? Anyway, like I said, sorry. I'm game to do the climb alone. See you when I get back.

Ty

P.S. My dad made it clear in the dream that he and your dad wanted to be together. You can thank me later!

It took a second for Ty's meaning to sink in. When it did, Cat reeled as if punched. "No," she moaned, "tell me you didn't . . ."

She stumbled to the living room. There on the mantel in the place where her father's ashes should have been was nothing but thin air.

Cat gasped. Maybe Aunt Lizzy could throw her climbing gear in Cascade Creek, move away, and put all reminders of Uncle Scott in the attic and forget about him. Maybe Aunt Lizzy could remarry and change her name. Maybe Aunt Lizzy didn't even care if Ty spread Uncle Scott's ashes on the mountain. But not Cat's mom. Hope Taylor had made it abundantly clear that she had no intention of ever leaving the log house she and Jonathan Taylor had built at the base of Storm Mountain. And his ashes would always, *always* be there with her, in remembrance.

True, it made Cat uneasy seeing her mother brush her hand across the urn as she walked by. And every now and then that uneasiness would build to the point where Cat would actually suggest that it might be time for Hope to get over Dad, move on with her life, be happy again, the way she used to be.

But words such as those, even gently delivered with the best of intentions, had plunged her mother back into a dark hole of despair. Imagine the effect of Dad's ashes gone, forever . . .

A sudden fury rose within Cat's core like magma in a volcano. Words caught in her throat, but when they finally erupted, they were white hot with indignation. "You have no right, Ty!"

The next thing she knew she was bolting from the house, Mugs at her heels. In seconds they were out the gravel driveway, across the road, and into forbidden territory.

"Thief!" Cat shouted, boots pounding up the steep switchbacks of Storm Mountain Trail. "Come back here!"

CHAPTER 4

ON SECOND THOUGHT

Outrage powered Cat more than two miles into the forest and gained her nearly fifteen hundred feet of elevation. Head down and arms pumping, she was so focused on catching Ty and retrieving her dad's ashes that she didn't see the trail sign until she nearly plowed into it.

Startled, she stepped back and stared at the small, weathered rectangle of wood bolted to a post at eye level. Carved into it were the words: BOUNDARY—STORM MOUNTAIN WILDERNESS.

Cat knew a lot about wilderness in general, but had a near encyclopedic load of information in her head about this wilderness in particular. Beyond that sign lay over forty-seven thousand acres—more than seventy-three square miles—of rugged, undeveloped mountain landscape. No roads, no houses, no schools, no McDonalds, no Walmart or Carmike Cinemas, no permanent human habitation of any kind. Set aside by an act of Congress in 1964, law required that everything within the wilderness remain as it had since the beginning of time, affected only by the forces of nature. People were allowed in, but only as visitors.

And only on wilderness terms, meaning self-reliance was the key. In other words, enter at your own risk.

Cat took in her surroundings. The forest at that altitude— over five thousand feet above sea level by now, she quickly figured, picturing the maps she'd memorized—was thick with mountain hemlock. Even though the sun was up, the light there under the dense evergreen canopy was dim, the shadows dark and suddenly ominous. The only sounds were those of the wind gusting through the boughs and her own labored breathing.

Despite the chill in the morning air, a rivulet of sweat dripped down the side of Cat's face. Primeval forests were just the beginning, she knew. The Storm Mountain Wilderness was also chockfull of deep canyons, roaring rivers, precarious boulder fields, towering cliffs, wild animals, and, of course, its namesake, the treacherous Storm Mountain itself.

Although it was still out of sight, Cat was sure she could feel the peak's presence. She ventured a quick glimpse upslope. That is when she noticed a small patch of snow. Only a few feet across, the remnant of winter was as much brown as it was white, sprinkled with twigs, conifer needles, and dust. The downhill edge was so saturated with meltwater, it was nearly translucent.

Still, Cat understood this was just a preview of what lay ahead. The higher she went, the more the landscape would defy the calendar. Rhododendron and cherry trees might be blooming in the valley, but in the high country, winter still ruled. Snow dominated. As she ascended, patches of it would grow larger and increasingly frequent, until it became deep and continuous. The ground would vanish altogether, as would the trail.

More snow could fall, too, any month of the year. A warm bluebird day—this very one, May 8, for example—could snap ugly in minutes. The mountaineering literature was full of such tales: gentle breezes suddenly morphing into icy fists, hammering the unsuspecting with a violence few could imagine; snow plastering the world white, blurring the line between earth and sky, especially above timberline. Especially high on the slopes of a peak like Storm Mountain, where fathers died. The patch of snow that lay in her path was evidence of that potential, its message doubly clear: Beware.

Cat looked away, only to find herself facing the Storm Mountain Wilderness boundary sign again, and all it implied. Hmmm . . . maybe, on second thought, chasing after crazy Cousin Ty wasn't such a good idea. Perhaps . . . no, probably . . . actually, *yes,* this was a job for the Storm County Sheriff's Department instead. There had been a theft—her famous father's ashes. It should be reported. Immediately. This was the right thing to do, for Mom's sake.

In one quick motion Cat pulled her cell phone from her pocket and flipped it open. She checked the display. No reception. Zero.

Holding her phone over her head, she pivoted a full three hundred sixty degrees, watching the bars. Still nothing. What was the deal? Even at her house, where reception was marginal, she could make a call. Here, not even a text message was possible.

Cat stopped. So then what was she doing? Not thinking, that's what she was doing. Keep your head screwed on straight, she lectured herself. If her phone didn't work in that location, the rational line of action was to go back home where it did and report the crime there. All she'd then have to do was wait for the sheriff to complete his job, and maybe have some breakfast in the meantime.

Mmmm, breakfast. Now that she thought about it, boy, was she hungry. No wonder. She'd gotten so wound up in wacko Ty's appearance last night that she'd forgotten to eat. And although her dad's pack was crammed with mountaineering gear—she checked it daily—there was no food.

Yes, emergency rations were on the Storm Mountain Search and Rescue Equipment Checklist she'd downloaded off their Web site. But in the two years since she'd inherited her father's pack, she'd never ventured farther with it than the backyard. It made no sense to stow snacks that would only go bad, and so there was not even one package of beef jerky inside, much less something really good, like a slice of homemade pesto pizza.

The image of her culinary masterpiece, still sitting on the kitchen counter where she'd left it, brought a rumble to Cat's stomach. Okay, so it might not be fresh out of the oven, but she bet it would still taste fantastic. After all, it was the best food in the world, especially when washed down with one of her home-made double-shot mochas. Leave right now and she could be home in thirty minutes. Once there she could call 9-1-1, then scarf every last crumb of that delectable treat. Cat nodded. Yep, good plan. Feed herself and Mugs, the pig-out king, too.

Speaking of Mugsy, where was he, anyway? Cat scanned the forest. "Mugs?"

She'd been so focused on catching Ty, she hadn't paid any attention to her dog. The last she remembered seeing him was at least fifteen minutes ago, probably more. He'd spotted a squirrel and, as usual, launched himself in hot pursuit.

Now Cat turned this way and that, calling. "Mugs? Hey, Mugs, where are you?"

Nothing.

She upped the volume. "Mugs! Here, boy!"

Again, nothing.

Cat peered into the shadows. "Mugs? C'mon, Mugs! Stop messing around and get back here! Don't play deaf on me!"

Still nothing.

The first wave of worry began to ripple deep in Cat's stomach. Why hadn't she put Mugs on a leash? She had the piece of climbing rope she used for practicing knots where she always kept it, right there in her pants pocket.

She pulled it out, as if to prove the fact of possession to herself, and quickly tied a figure-eight follow-through. How easy it would have been to cinch Mugs to her in the same way. How stupid not to! She crammed the rope back into her pocket, all set to scream Mugs's name.

That's when she heard the distant yet unmistakable howl of a husky. It came from the total opposite direction Cat wished to go—deep inside the wilderness area, high on Storm Mountain.

CHAPTER 5

NORTH FACE DIRECT

"Aw, Mugs," Cat moaned. She kicked at a tree root. "Not now! We need to get home!"

Home. Cat turned back down the trail in that direction, and for an instant the powerful urge to beat a hasty retreat nearly overwhelmed her.

In the next instant she stopped. Go home and what? Abandon her dog? The way he'd been abandoned as a puppy?

Cat winced at the thought. She could still vividly remember the evening two years ago, a few days after the memorial service was over and all the well-wishers had at last gone away. To Cat's great relief, her mother finally stopped crying, took a deep breath, and got up off the couch. "We're going to town for groceries," she announced. And so they did.

Shopping cart loaded, mother and daughter were pushing it across Richie's IGA parking lot toward their car when Cat heard a weak whimper. She looked up, expecting it to be her mom breaking down once more. But no, thank goodness, Hope's eyes were still dry, and she had heard it, too.

The whimper came again. They followed the sound to a nearby Dumpster. Kneeling on the gritty pavement, they looked underneath to discover a wet, shivering puppy cowering beside an empty milk carton.

Cat gently pulled the stray to her and tucked it into her coat. She curled her body over it and looked down into its sad brown eyes. "Hi, little guy," she said, and was rewarded with a sloppy kiss on the end of her nose.

Hope started crying again, and Cat had to look away. But her mom said she could keep the puppy. Cat named it Mugs, after her father's hero, the great mountaineer Mugs Stump.

Now Cat kicked at the tree root again, but this time in frustration at herself. How could she even *think* of leaving Mugs behind? He didn't know how to fend for himself at home, much less in the middle of an unmerciful wilderness. Imagine all that could happen!

A wave of disturbing possibilities crashed into Cat's brain:

Mugs lost in the shadowy forest, wandering helplessly.

Mugs stumbling, tangled in underbrush, or struggling on rocky ground, exhausted.

Mugs whining with hunger.

Mugs caught out in the cold blackness of a moonless night, trembling under a log.

Mugs's yelp of terror as a mountain lion pounced.

Cat shuddered. That's right, this was cougar country. True, they were extremely rare. You could wander the forest for an entire lifetime and never spot one. But what if . . . ?

"No," Cat said aloud, "don't go there." She pushed back the image of bared fangs and claws. Focus! She needed to find her dog, return to the house, and call the sheriff. She could still get Dad's ashes back on the mantel before Mom came home from the conference on Sunday, no problem. Hope would never need to know.

Cat cinched her dad's pack tighter around her waist and shoulders, then slowly turned and faced uphill. "Mugs!" she called, venturing a first step past the boundary sign and into the Storm Mountain Wilderness. "Hey, Mugs!"

Surely he would show up any second, and they could head home together.

"Here, Mugs! C'mon, boy!"

Surely.

A half hour later Cat was still searching, now for both her dog and the trail, which had vanished under the snowpack as she gained elevation. She stopped to consider her options. Reason suggested that without a marked path she might as well head straight in the direction where she'd last heard Mugs's howl—directly uphill. Cat did not argue with reason.

This straight-line approach worked fine, for about ten steps. At which point Cat's feet shot out from under her on the steepening slope, and she ended up facedown with a mouthful of snow.

An ice ax and crampons were the logical solution. It took

a few frustrating minutes to remember how to get the spikes strapped securely on to her boots, and how to hold her dad's old wooden-shaft ax, the first he'd ever owned, and so her favorite. Still, the initial results seemed promising.

Until she caught a crampon point on her pant leg and tripped. Flailing to regain her balance, she nearly stabbed herself in the thigh with the sharp pick of the ax—and ended up face-first in the snow, again.

"C'mon, Cat," she muttered to herself. "You know how to do this!"

Stepping more cautiously, she finally got the hang of it. It was hard work, though, especially when she encountered a section of softer snow and sank shin-deep. Once she plunged in up to her hip. Which—just to keep things interesting—got her not only another mouthful of snow but an earful, too.

Fighting off mounting frustration, Cat continued calling for Mugs and climbing higher. Soon mountain hemlock gave way to subalpine fir. She found herself fighting her way through a particularly dense stand of it when her pack strap caught on a limb and jerked her off her feet, slamming her backward onto the snow. She lay there like a boxer down for the count.

"Aw, give me a break," she complained. What was this, the eighth time she'd gone instantly horizontal? Well, okay, only the fourth. Still, it seemed like she was more down than up!

Plus, there was the souvenir bruise on her arm. *And* the scrape on her elbow. *And* the sore throat from calling, calling, and calling for Mugs. All to no avail. No dog found.

Not yet, anyway.

Cat struggled to her feet. "Mugs?" She resumed pushing her way through the thicket of fir only to have a bough snap back and slap her across the cheek. "Ow!" She lurched away from the sting, hit another limb, lurched again. It was as if the trees were on the attack, trying to hold her prisoner.

Frustration turned to renewed anger at Ty—this was all his fault!—and a sudden surge of adrenaline. "Enough!" Cat barked. She lowered her head and charged uphill. Branches clawed at her. She fought her way forward with all her might. The limbs bent, letting out a chorus of cracks. All at once they gave way. She shot out of the trees and went hurtling toward a wall of solid stone. She spun at the last second and, instead of slamming face-first into it, ended up facedown in the snow. Number five.

"Good grief," Cat moaned. "What now?" She looked up to find that she had almost butted heads with a boulder the size of a school bus. Against it, around to the left, leaned another stone—not as large, but still as big as a car propped on end. Together the two formed an improbable steeple-shaped doorway large enough for a grown man to pass through.

Cat immediately recognized the chance combination of rock coming to rest on rock from the photos she kept in her filing cabinet. They, and in particular the passageway between them, formed the benchmark climbers used when descending Storm Mountain's north side. The boulders had no official name, and didn't even show on the topographic maps, but climbers knew the passage between them as the Hallelujah Gate. Miss it and you could wander below into the wrong drainage and end up hopelessly lost in the forest. Get it in your sights and—hallelujah!—you'd found the right way off the north side of Storm Mountain.

Cat stood and leaned into the largest of the two boulders for a moment to rest, then plodded over to the Hallelujah Gate and looked through. Her breath caught in her throat.

She was at timberline, roughly six thousand feet of elevation in the Oregon Cascades, at which point forest gave way to the alpine zone. Below the Hallelujah Gate trees thrived. Above it only a few small islands of stunted, weather-ravaged subalpine firs remained. Beyond those rugged holdouts the landscape quickly steepened into a barren world of snow and rock and ice. Then it steepened even more, drawing the eye upward.

In her regular life at home, and at school in town, it had always been fairly easy for Cat to brush off Storm Mountain as nothing more than a dormant volcano, a big, glaciated pile of igneous rocks. And although on clear days the peak's upper reaches could be spotted on the horizon from as much as one hundred miles away, she had made a point to block out what had happened to her father on its flanks. If the mountain crept into her line of sight, she would quickly avert her gaze and move on.

Now, though, Storm Mountain was no longer a distant tri-angle of white or a photo in a climbing guide book. It loomed above her, massive beyond belief, unavoidable.

And much more than a glaciated pile of igneous rock. Its vast snowfields, sweeping skyward from where she stood, seemed like monstrous dragon's wings. The Hood Glacier, which twisted its way from the base of the North Face, could be a dragon's tongue. And the summit—she had to tilt her head back to take it all in—the summit jutted above a collar of swirling gray clouds, stabbing the sky like a cruel dragon's head. The mountain felt alive and angry, as if it were about to rear up and pounce on any who dared trespass.

Cat shuddered and tried in vain to pry her eyes away. She stared helplessly, openmouthed, transfixed, and suddenly compelled. She had to find the spot. Had to!

Dropping her gaze from the dragon's-head pinnacle, Cat scanned the North Face of the mountain—over cornices, windscoured ridges, gouged avalanche chutes, bands of black vertical rock. Until she stopped abruptly at a towering thousand-foot headwall. She narrowed her field of vision, searching for what she dreaded and yet felt driven to find.

When she saw the narrow line of ice that cleaved the headwall from top to bottom, she knew. She'd read the climbing guidebooks dozens of times and pored over the photos with a magnifying glass, burning this particular route into her memory. Yes, there was no doubt. That was the famous North Face Direct, unanimously considered among alpinists to be the most daring and dangerous climb on Storm Mountain. It had been pioneered and first ascended by none other than Jonathan and Scott Taylor. And it was right . . . there, on an exposed narrow ledge about halfway up, that they had been trapped by the storm during the rescue mission and dug that tiny snow cave where they died.

At the sight of the exact location of the tragedy, Cat's vision went glassy. For a moment she felt weak in the knees, dizzy, and teetered as if on the edge of an abyss. Nausea threatened. She jammed her father's ice ax shaft into the snow and bent forward, leaning on it to steady herself.

It took three ragged breaths for her head to clear. Gingerly she pushed herself upright, just in time to catch a tiny, distant movement on the mountainside.

"Mugs?"

Cat yanked her backpack off and dropped it onto the snow. She pulled her father's powerful Nikon binoculars from the top pouch and quickly zeroed in on Backbone Spur, the lateral moraine that ran alongside the western flank of the Hood Glacier.

The first thing that came into focus was a cornice of wind-sculpted snow thrusting like a frozen wave from the crest of Backbone Spur out over the ice field. Scanning upslope from there, she spotted a speck of neon orange, a blot of red.

Neon orange like a stocking cap.

Red as Uncle Scott's mountain parka.

Ty.

At the sight of her cousin, Cat stiffened. "You!" The heat of anger rose in her face. She dialed in the binoculars for better focus.

There. Ty stood on a small mound of snow holding something out at arm's length, jiggling it the way a fisherman does bait.

Below him, leaping up for what *had* to be some kind of food, was a chowhound husky.

CHAPTER 6

OR ELSE

Relief and amazement flooded Cat at the same time. Relief at seeing Mugs alive and well. Amazement that he could sniff out grub at such a distance and follow his nose to it. Sure, she'd read that dogs could sense odors at concentrations 110 *million* times lower than humans, but still, in the middle of a wilderness?

No matter. Mugs's supersnout wasn't the point. The point was that Ty had not only stolen her dad's ashes, he'd also lured her dog up the mountain.

Cat's face went hot. "Ty!"

No response. Through the binoculars she could see him dangling his food bait over Mugs's head.

"Get down here!" She willed him with her mind to look her way, commanded him to descend with that ridiculous, gaudy stocking cap in hand, apologies streaming, and deliver the stolen goods.

Ty stayed arrogantly perched on the crest of Backbone Spur. "Ty!" Cat yelled. "Don't make me come up there!"

Really. She'd do it. She swore she would. If he could climb that high on Storm Mountain, she could, too. She wasn't afraid!

Once again, no response. Cat fumed, then got control. Think! Focus! Dogs not only had better noses than humans, they also possessed better ears. If Mugs heard her, and for once in his life came when called, then maybe, just maybe, Ty would follow with the ashes. Two problems solved in one swoop. "Mugs!" she shouted. "Come, Mugsy! Here, boy!"

Through the binoculars Cat saw Mugs leap again for the food Ty jiggled.

Cat tried barking. "Arf! Arf!" Then howling like Mugs did when he saw a squirrel on the bird feeder. "*Ah-ooo!*" Maybe dog language would alert him.

Still nothing. But then, what did she expect? Even if the sound waves of her noisemaking were actually reaching Mugs's ears, they wouldn't penetrate to the brain. When it came to food, Mugs was deaf to all else.

Cat zeroed in again with the binoculars just as Ty dropped some bait to Mugs. Whatever the treat was, it was a hit. Mugs lunged and scarfed it down in seconds, then looked back up to Ty for another helping. Ty threw back his head, laughing. In the next moment, apparently tired of fishing-for-dogs, he grabbed his pack up off the snow and slung it over his shoulders.

"That's right," Cat coaxed as she watched. "Come to your

senses. Bring me my dad's ashes and my dog right now, or else I'll—*What? Don't!*"

Cat watched in disbelief as Ty motioned to Mugs, then together the two started climbing *up,* not down. He not only meant to continue his ascent of Storm Mountain, he was headed straight up Backbone Spur toward the base of the North Face and the beginning of the North Face Direct route. Cat had assumed he would traverse to the east and ascend the Dog Walk Ridge, so-called because it was the easiest route to the top. Yes, it was longer. Climbers regularly misjudged the time required and got stuck in the dark. "Benighted" it was called, and resulted in an uncomfortable bivouac. Or sometimes a rescue. But to attempt the North Face Direct? With Mugs in tow? This was beyond illogical, way past crazy. It was suicidal!

As if to punctuate Cat's point, a muffled crack sounded from higher on the mountain. Cat looked up to see a huge chunk of ice breaking away at the top of the North Face. It tumbled down, knocking off more snow and ice as it went, until it had grown into a giant white wave that crashed onto the upper reaches of the Hood Glacier with a roar.

"Good grief!" Cat whispered. She focused again with the binoculars. Surely an avalanche would turn Ty back. . . . No! He was still headed up.

Panic surged. That avalanche had barely missed Backbone Spur. What if the next one didn't? She *had* to get their attention! But how? *Think!*

Cat's mind raced. Of course, her emergency whistle! Why

hadn't she thought of that before? She grabbed it from the top pouch of her pack and blew hard. The shrillness stabbed her ears. She winced. Like much of her father's equipment, she had examined the whistle dozens of times, knew its purpose, history, and every detail, but had never actually given it more than a trial toot. Now she held it in her mouth and covered her ears with her hands, then blew again, long and hard. The wind gusted and swept the piercing sound of the whistle away. Neither Ty nor Mugs reacted. They hadn't heard a thing.

Cat looked up the mountain again. The weather was deteriorating fast. Clouds that minutes ago had only ringed the summit had since thickened and completely blocked it from view. Swirling fingers of gray raked across the North Face, descending.

Dragon breath.

Cat had no choice. She had to catch Ty before he reached the North Face headwall and got both himself and her dog killed. She swooped up her pack and ice ax, and, fists clenched, charged out of the Hallelujah Gate.

CHAPTER 7

INTO THE DRAGON'S LAIR

Distance is a hard thing to judge in a vast mountain landscape. Cat knew this from her readings. Still, she was surprised when after thirty minutes of pursuit it seemed she'd hardly gained any ground on Ty at all. What she'd imagined to be a speedy mission to nab the villain and retrieve the stolen goods was not going as planned.

Especially given the fact that she was gasping for breath, her heart was pounding, and her legs were beginning to go Gumby on her. She felt like she was slogging through mashed potatoes with lead weights on her feet. In frustration she pushed even harder, but within seconds came to a staggering stop.

Think, she reminded herself. Up here on the mountain, the air was thinner. Which meant less oxygen per breath. Which, in turn, meant fatigue. What had Dad and the books said about climbing at altitude? She took a deep breath and focused. Despite her fierce drive to overtake Ty, she needed to be the tortoise, not the hare. Slow and steady would catch the crook. She ramped down her pace and began to use what mountaineers call the rest step—a momentary pause with each footfall before pushing on. Step, rest, step, rest. That was the cadence needed. Step, rest, step.

Quickly Cat's breathing fell in rhythm with her feet. With every stride she exhaled forcefully. With each momentary pause to rest, she inhaled. This was pressure breathing, another mountaineering trick.

"Step, breath, rest." Cat said aloud, punching out air, then drawing it in. "Step, breath, rest."

Soon her heart slowed to a more manageable rate, and her legs perked up a bit, too. "Step, breath, rest." It was working!

Jabbing her ice ax into the snow, kicking with crampon points, Cat moved steadily now, gaining altitude. The slope steepened. She adjusted her tempo accordingly, slowing even more, and tried not to think about the North Face looming above her, another avalanche, or the dire consequences of a simple misjudgment. No worries, she told herself. She wasn't climbing Storm Mountain. No one was setting foot on the North Face Direct. This was a police action, the right thing to do, for Mugs's sake, and her mom's.

True, she could no longer see her criminal cousin and runaway dog. They had moved behind a knoll on the crest of Backbone Spur. And the clouds had lowered even more.

Still, Ty knew nothing about climbing, the rest step, or pressure breathing. He had rejected Uncle Scott's offers to teach him a mountaineer's ways. Now he was racing ahead, impulsive, not thinking about where he was going, like when he was a kid and ran right off the edge of the bank and into Cascade

Creek. No doubt he was stopping to catch his breath, and feed Mugs, and who knew what else.

Which was just like him, Cat thought. He had always been easily distracted. Get a good game of search-and-rescue going when they were kids, and within seconds Ty would be playing pirates vs. Godzilla or let's-go-swing-from-that-tree-limb. Illogical, hyper, scatterbrained, he had driven her crazy.

Now, though, Ty's faults were working in Cat's favor. Logic and relentless pursuit would win out over impulse, girl drive over boy randomness.

Step, breath, rest. Step, breath, rest.

Higher and higher Cat climbed, into the descending clouds. She forced her mind off the deteriorating visibility, the steepening terrain, the history of Storm Mountain she knew all too well. Dwelling on it would only make her lose sight of her goal.

Step, breath, rest. Step, breath, rest.

Then the angle of the slope eased, and Cat looked up to see that she had reached the crest of Backbone Spur. She was greeted by a powerful gust of wind out of the west, carrying with it a cold bite that raised instant goose bumps on her skin. She unshouldered her pack and pulled out a jacket, knit cap, and gloves. In the few seconds it took to do this, the wind gusted again, even stronger, sweeping the clouds back off the ridge. Cat looked out to see the abrupt west side of the spur for the first time up close. It dropped away from her in a headlong, pell-mell dive that didn't stop for at least two hundred feet, where it reached the Hood Glacier below.

Cat stopped short, jacket halfway zipped, and gaped. She had read much about glaciers, and knew that although they looked solid, they were actually a very slow-moving river of ice. Global warming was causing them to shrink all around the world. In Africa on Mount Kilimanjaro, the famous snows were almost gone. The Hood Glacier here on Storm Mountain had shrunk, too. Photos showed it to be two-thirds the length it had been just a century ago. Still, seeing it this close and from this aerial perspective, the tongue of ice looked massive. And dangerous. Beneath the snowy surface lay hidden cracks in the ice called crevasses, many up to one hundred feet deep.

Jonathan and Scott Taylor had been as comfortable on the Hood Glacier as most people were on a sidewalk. They had loved to play in those crevasses in the late summer and autumn when the snow bridges had cleared, practicing rescue techniques or just ice climbing for fun.

Cat had a photo on her bedroom wall of her father scaling the vertical wall of a particularly large crevasse. It had always given her chills to look at it, to imagine what it would be like to be in the belly of the beast, held in place by only those tiny metal crampon front points and the slender picks of ice axes, just a slip away from plummeting.

Sure, her dad and uncle always put in ice screws to hold the rope in case of a fall. But screws sometimes pulled. Car-size chunks of ice could suddenly let loose, too, pancaking a climber in a heartbeat.

That's what had happened to Dad's hero, Mugs Stump. He'd

been descending the South Buttress of Denali in Alaska when he went over to check on a crevasse that blocked the way. The lip of the crevasse collapsed with him on it and crushed him beneath tons of ice. His body was never recovered.

Cat remembered Dad telling the story one night at the dinner table. He'd been matter-of-fact about it, sure it wouldn't happen to him. He had a family to come home to.

"And speaking of family," he had then said, "I'm going to take you up on the Hood Glacier, Cat, and teach you the ropes as soon as you turn thirteen!"

Cat had beamed at the thought of such a rite of passage. "Cool!" But now that she was thirteen and looking down onto the glacier for the first time, the reality of it didn't feel so cool. The image of giant collapsing teeth of ice made her stomach tighten into a knot.

The wind gusted again. Clouds closed back in over Backbone Spur, obscuring the Hood Glacier below. Cat shivered and finished zipping up her jacket, then turned to find footprints—both dog and human—and scraps of cheese and a couple of beans just a few steps from where she stood.

At the sight of the crime scene, a rankling burn returned to Cat's gut. She faced up Backbone Spur, ready to scream Ty's name at the top of her lungs, when she picked up a faint sound. Was that . . . hip-hop?

The wind flared again, raking cold fingers across the ridge. Cat peered intently into the icy fog as a singing, dancing figure and a husky emerged out of the gloom.

CHAPTER 8

THE END

Ty's face lit up into a big grin when he saw Cat. "Hey! I thought Mugs had followed me on his own, but you changed your mind and came, too! Cool! Just like old times, you and me together."

He spread his arms in welcome as he moved closer. The dog bait Cat had seen from a distance was still in his hand—a grease-soaked brown paper bag. It swung low, stopping right over Mugs's head. Mugs locked in on the opening and leaped.

With a hoot of laughter, Ty jerked the bag back. "What a pig you are!" he chided. "I already gave you three burritos and you act like you're starving!"

Cat stood, glaring.

For all the good it did. Ty didn't seem to notice. He was too busy lecturing on Mexican cuisine.

"True, I'll grant you, we're not just talking any old burrito here." He patted the bag for emphasis. "These were imported by yours truly all the way from Ricardo's Taco Shop in Seattle. They may be a day old, but they're still primo—refried beans layered with shredded cheddar cheese, then topped off with tons of pico de gallo salsa. Su-weet! Best food on the planet, especially when washed down with an ample supply of Mountain Dew."

He grinned. "Not that I've got any of the golden elixir with me. I mean, who would be stupid enough to lug a six-pack of it all the way up here? But Ricardo's tacos? Worth every ounce of the load, right, Mugs?"

Eyes riveted on Ty's food bag, Mugs wagged his tail furiously.

Ty shook his head. "When I first saw him flying up the mountain like a dog possessed, I thought that he was just glad to see *me*. Ha! He was just glad to see *food*! I leaned over to say hi and he snatched a burrito right out of my hand! Scarfed it down in one bite, *todus porkus,* whole hog!"

Ty made an oinking sound, then laughed. "You should have seen him, Cat!" He looked his cousin's way again, and this time her glare registered. His grin faded. "Uh-oh," he said. "What's wrong?"

"That's *my* dog," Cat growled.

For a long moment Ty stared, apparently uncomprehending. Another surge of wind raced across Backbone Spur, driving the clouds with it. Ty's parka flapped like a flag. Finally he mumbled, "What?"

"I said, 'That's *my* dog.' He belongs with *me*!"

To prove it, Cat marched over, snow flying with each emphatic step. She yanked her practice rope from her pocket and quickly tied one end to Mugs's collar with a figure-eight follow-through.

The other end she tied in the same fashion to a belt loop at her hip, then leveled dagger eyes on Ty.

"Now give me my dad's ashes, you thief!"

Ty flinched as if slapped. "Thief?"

"You *stole* my dad's ashes! That makes you a *thief*!"

Ty shook his head. "No way. I told you about my dream, remember? I thought—"

"Whatever you thought or dreamed up is *wrong*!" Cat shot back.

"Aw, c'mon," Ty said, pleading now. "Our dads were more than just twins, you know that. They did everything together. And were always there for each other. When your dad had that gnarly mountain bike wreck, my dad gave blood. When my dad needed a kidney, your dad donated one of his. But most of all, they were climbing partners. They trusted each other with their lives. It's only right that their ashes should be spread together. I was sure you would understand."

"Here's what *you'd* better understand," Cat said. She whipped her cell phone from her pocket and flipped it open. Now that she was above timberline and out in the open, she had reception. It wasn't great—only two bars—but it was good enough. She pointed the phone at her cousin as if it were a gun. "You can't come barging into my life and do whatever you feel like. Give my dad's ashes back in the next nanosecond or I'm calling nine-one-one and siccing the cops on you!"

Ty gawked, wide-eyed.

"*Nine . . .*" Cat said, punching the number dramatically with her index finger. "*One . . .*"

Ty's shoulders slumped. He held up his hands as if under arrest. "Okay, okay, put the phone away. I'll give you your dad's ashes."

Cat slipped her cell phone back in her pocket but kept her hand at the ready. She watched Ty's every move as he unshouldered his pack, unclipped the top pouch, and pulled the main compartment open.

"Look, I'm sorry," he said. "I had no idea you'd get so bent out of shape. I thought I was doing you and your mom a favor." He blew out a puff of air and shrugged. "Oh well, good thing I turned around when I did, huh?"

Now it was Cat's turn to gawk. "*Turned around?* Do you mean to tell me you are headed back down the mountain?"

"Well, yeah," Ty said as if this were a given. "The weather is turning nasty, and the clouds got thicker the higher I went. I couldn't see very well, and I figured I'd get stranded up there and need to be rescued, which would be embarrassing. Who needs *that.*"

He laughed. "And then there was the avalanche. Did you see that thing come down off the mountain? The more I thought about it, the more I thought, *Whoa!* Anyway, you get the point. Not a good day for spreading ashes. But, hey, the mountain will still be here tomorrow. It may not be May eighth, but close enough. I'll come back then. Dad won't mind, as long as I get the job done."

Cat couldn't answer. She was too busy trying to process what she'd just heard. And what it meant—that all of the trouble, and worry, and hard work chasing Ty up the mountain was for . . . nothing. She could have sat home eating pesto pizza and drinking mochas and simply waited. Ty would have eventually showed up with the stolen goods.

Cat shook her head. If only her seventh-grade humanities teacher, Mr. Hines, could see this. He had tried and tried to get the concept of irony across to the class. Most hadn't cared. Cat just hadn't gotten it, until now. So *this* was what he'd meant when he'd written on the white board, "Irony: The incongruity between an expectation and what actually happens." Now the effect was so ridiculous, it made her laugh, but there was absolutely no humor in it. "Give me my dad's ashes," she said. "And hurry it up."

Ty nodded. *"Sí, señorita."* He reached into his pack and pulled an urn out into the light. The brushed brass glinted as he turned it over and examined the writing on the bottom.

"Oops," he said. "Wrong one. This is *my* dad."

With great care he set his father's ashes aside, making sure the urn was situated so it wouldn't slide downhill on the snow. That done, he dug Jonathan Taylor's remains from his pack. He cradled the urn close for a moment in the crook of his arm. "Really, I'm sorry, Cat. I thought spreading their ashes would be a good thing."

"Yeah, well it's *not*," Cat said, drilling her words into him.

Ty's eyes narrowed for an instant, but then softened. He held out the urn. "Here you go," he said, his voice trailing off into a whisper of resignation.

Cat started to reach for her father's ashes, then stopped short. Although she had studied the urn hundreds of times as it sat on the mantel at home, and imagined in detail how it might feel to run her fingers over the smooth, cool brass, the truth was that she had never actually been able to bring herself to touch it. Mom did pretty much every day, and often picked it up, dusted it, adjusted its position ever so slightly. But not Cat. She had always kept her distance.

Now she quickly took her backpack off and opened the main compartment wide. "Put it in here," she said.

Ty looked down into the pack, then up at Cat. He cocked his head in the same way Mugs often did and studied her face. The wind flared again, driving the icy fog before it.

Cat fought off a shiver. "Put it in here," she repeated. What was it with him? Did she have to say everything a dozen times? She shoved the open pack at him.

Ty hesitated for a moment more, then gently placed the urn inside. "All yours."

"That's right," Cat said. "All mine." To emphasize the point, she yanked the pack drawcord tight, closing off the urn. She snapped the top pouch down over it and pulled the compression straps snug. Load secured, she swung it onto her back. Story over. Search and rescue mission accomplished.

In other words, The End.

And Ty?

Cat shot her crazy thief-of-a-cousin a quick glance.

Ty could do whatever he wanted.

Without another word, Cat turned away and headed down the mountain. She did not look back.

CHAPTER 9

GOING, GOING . . .

Gravity and relief worked in Cat's favor. She quickly settled into a steady, loping gait as she moved down the crest of Backbone Spur, swinging her feet out far in front of her, letting her heels hit first and sink into the softening snow. Her ice ax swung lazily at her side. The clouds were thinning with every step she descended. Soon she'd see the Hallelujah Gate pointing the way home.

Mugs trotted beside her on the end of the practice-rope leash, apparently over his burrito fixation. Burrito out of sight, burrito out of doggy mind.

Cat lectured him anyway, because it kept her mind and her eyes off the precipitous drop to her left and the twisted Hood Glacier below. And because grousing lifted her mood. "Some friend you are!" she said. "After all I've done for you, you desert me and go chasing up the mountain to gobble a . . . a *burrito*? Best food in the world? No way!"

Mugs sidled closer and wagged his tail. Cat wagged her finger.

49

"You should have come when I called. What's with you? You go deaf when you smell food?"

Cat fumed as she heard Ty from back up the ridge. She wasn't able to make out what he was saying with all the wind, but just the insistent sound of his voice set her off. He'd had that annoying habit as a kid, too, always needing to get in the last word.

"I ought to call the cops on him," she grumbled. "Even though we got the ashes back, that doesn't change the fact that they were ripped off in the first place. Yeah, I should, just to teach him to keep his nose out of other people's business."

Ty called again. Cat could hear urgency in his voice.

"No way, Cousin," she said. "What do you think I am, some kind of fool who—"

A muffled whump beneath Cat's feet cut her short. She looked down to see a jagged crack shoot out across the surface of the snow. In the next instant the solid world where she and Mugs were standing abruptly broke into pieces and began to slide.

Avalanche! The realization ripped through Cat's brain. Every cell in her body jolted with fear and adrenaline. She twisted toward stable ground and dug her father's ice ax in, just as she'd been taught.

Too little, too late. Her feet were yanked out from under her, the ax jerked from her hands. More snow broke loose. Everything accelerated. In seconds she was plunging down the steep western slope of Backbone Spur.

From somewhere to the side, Cat heard Mugs yelp, and knew in a flash that the avalanche had ripped out her belt loop and taken her dog and the leash with it, figure-eight follow-through and all.

"Mugs!" Cat shouted, craning her neck. For an instant she saw him and the terror in his eyes, but before she could reach out for him, she was slammed in the back by a fist of snow and pushed under.

The world went dark. Blocks of wet snow pummeled her from all sides. She tumbled as if tossed by a giant ocean wave. Crashing, spinning, Cat couldn't tell up from down. Snow crammed between her pack and her back, down her collar, up her jacket sleeves, even up her nostrils. It filled her mouth.

Gagging, frantic for air, Cat grabbed blindly, pulling, swimming, clawing to get to the surface, but seemed to just sink deeper.

The avalanche began to slow. Cat knew that once it stopped, it would set like concrete within seconds, clamping her in a frigid vise. Her only chance of survival was to get her hands up in front of her face to create space for a pocket of air. Without it her warm breath would glaze over the snow, creating a "death mask," and she'd quickly suffocate on her own carbon dioxide. She tried to force her arms up, but they were pinned to her sides.

The snow slowed more. Cat shuddered with a horrible realization. When it mattered most, all that Dad had taught her and all that she'd read and committed to memory meant nothing.

Like a fool, she had walked right into the dragon's trap. Now she was going to die in a tomb of white on exactly the same day as her father had died two years before. The grief would surely kill her mother.

Stupid, she thought as the dragon's fist closed in on her. Stupid, stupid, stupid.

CHAPTER 10

. . . GONE

At the last second the avalanche shifted and a glimmer of light shone from above. With it Cat felt a burst of hope. She wrenched upward with all her might. Her head and one arm broke the surface. In a violent heave she retched out the snow clogging her throat. Agonizing gasps filled her lungs with blessed air just as the avalanche stopped moving.

"Cat!" From behind her Cat heard a frantic voice and crashing footsteps. "Hold on, I'm coming!"

Panting, heart pounding with adrenaline, Cat looked up through a blurred haze to see Ty racing down the slope of Backbone Spur toward her. He tripped and fell over a block of the fanned-out avalanche debris but was back on his feet in an instant, and then hovering over her.

"Are you okay?"

Cat tried to speak, but nothing came out. The world was spinning, her head roaring.

"I was yelling!" Ty said. "I was yelling and yelling at you to watch out for that overhanging thing of snow. What do you call it? Oh, yeah, a cornice. I tried to warn you about walking out on that cornice, but . . . never mind. Let's get you out of there."

Ty began pulling chunks of hardened snow away from Cat, quickly freeing both her arms. She told herself to help dig, but it was useless. Her fumbling fingers simply would not cooperate.

"Relax, I'll do the work," Ty said. Soon he had her clear to the waist and had cleaned the snow out of her collar and from between her pack and her back.

"Good enough," he announced. He moved around behind Cat and grabbed her under the arms. "Ready?" he said, and, without waiting for an answer, heaved.

For a moment, Cat felt like her legs were going to tear off, but then the avalanche's grip broke and Ty fell backward, hauling her out onto the surface of the snow with him.

"Whoa!" Ty said with a laugh. "That was like popping a cork . . . sort of."

Dizzy, dazed, numb, Cat pushed herself up onto her knees, only to immediately collapse back on the avalanche debris like a punctured balloon. She lay there shaking, and yet oddly stunned with wonder. Look how far the avalanche had carried her—all the way down Backbone Spur and at least fifty yards out onto the surface of the Hood Glacier. And yet the slide had been a small one, and she'd been pushed to the side where the flow was slower and not so deep. And—most miraculously—she had survived. Yeah, she'd lost her ice ax and her knit cap. But no body parts were broken. Look!

Legs?

Yep. Still attached.

Arms?

Check.

Head?

Well, yes, although many would question it, considering how stupid she'd been to get caught in the first place.

But who cared? She was alive! Alive, and she still had her dad's pack on her back. Which meant the ashes were still safely inside.

Cat burst into a cropped, manic fit of laughter, as if she'd just gotten off a roller coaster. She'd cheated death. She was breathing and all in one piece. Amazing!

A desperate, muffled whine cut all thoughts of celebration short. "Mugs?" How could she have forgotten? She struggled to her feet, eyes darting. "MUGS?"

Ty was already up and calling, "*HERE, BOY!*"

The whine came again, from behind them. Ty and Cat both spun to see a gray-and-white tail sticking out of the jumble of avalanche debris.

"Mugs!" they both shouted. Ty rushed toward the buried dog. Cat stumbled after him.

"Hold on, Mugs," Ty said. "We'll get you out of there!"

They both dug at the blocks of snow, Ty hammering them with his fists, throwing broken pieces over his shoulder.

Mugs cried out.

"Almost there!" Cat said, clawing at the remaining chunks.

"Yeah, almost there!" Ty chimed in. He levered the last piece free, sending it flying. "Yes!" He reached down and, with a grunt, pulled the trembling dog into his arms. The practice-rope leash that had ripped from Cat's belt loop dangled from Mugs's collar, still tied with a figure-eight follow-through.

"Come on, big guy," Ty said. "Let's get away from this bad-boy avalanche." He stood, staggered under the weight of his load, but then righted himself and lurched off the field of debris and onto the smooth surface of the glacier. Still reeling and disoriented, Cat lumbered after him. With Ty, it seemed, she was always bringing up the rear.

"Hey," she managed to croak. "He's my dog. I want to hold him."

Ty seemed not to have heard. He hugged Mugs close. "Saved ya!" he crowed. Until he lost his balance and, laughing, pitched sideways into a shallow ditch in the snow.

A dim light flickered on in Cat's addled head. Something was wrong with this picture. But what? She blinked and tried to focus, take in more of her surroundings. The depression Ty and Mugs lay in was not wide—maybe only ten feet—but, she now realized, very long, arcing out across the surface of the glacier for at least a hundred yards. It was if the snow had . . . sagged. But why would it do that?

Then the light flashed on, and with it a blaring alarm. "You're on a snow bridge!" she yelled, rushing toward Ty and Mugs.

"There's a crevasse right under you!" She jumped in and reached for her dog. "We need to get off of here as fast as—"

The snow creaked beneath them. Mugs yelped and clawed free of Ty's arms, then sprang up onto solid footing. Cat whirled and lunged for the same spot, but it was too late. The horizontal world of the glacier went suddenly vertical. Cat and Ty plummeted straight down into the mouth of the dragon.

CHAPTER 11

MADE YOU LOOK!

Cat's back arched. Her mind shrieked in terror. And yet only a gasp escaped her mouth. She hit a sloping ledge, tumbled, and was airborne again.

But just for a heartbeat. She bashed into a wall, spun in mid-air, then slammed onto a shelf of ice, which knocked the wind from her. An instant later Ty thudded down beside her with a sharp grunt that echoed in the crevasse.

From above, Mugs let out a shrill yip. As Cat twisted around to look up for him, the pain in her left knee registered. It was as if the joint had burst into searing flames. She found her voice and loosed it in a piercing scream.

Reflexively, she clutched her knee, but the movement sent an excruciating jolt through her entire leg. She screamed again.

"Cat? What?"

Cat looked over in the dim light of the crevasse to see Ty kneeling beside her.

"What's hurt?"

Cat could only answer with yet another scream. It felt like a giant hand was wrenching her knee out of its socket. She pulled her pant leg up and cried out at the sight. "It's broken!"

Ty leaned close. "Nope, not broken; the kneecap is just dislocated, that's all. See how it's pushed over to the side? Yep, dislocated kneecap. No doubt about it."

In the midst of such suffering—miles beyond any Cat had ever experienced—anger came roaring back with a vengeance. "So now you're a doctor?" she shouted.

Ty seemed unfazed. "No, just a soccer player. Or at least I was until I dislocated my kneecap, just like yours. Twice. That's why I quit. Hasn't happened since. But I still know a dislocation when I see one, and I know how to put it back in. It's simple." He started to reach for her. "Just relax and—"

"*Relax?*" Cat stared in furious disbelief. "Look at what you've gotten us into!" Above them rose twenty feet of near vertical, glistening blue ice, capped by the snow bridge, which was broken only by the hole they'd created when they'd fallen through. It framed the white light of day and the silhouette of Mugs's head as he peered down at them and barked. Below, past the narrow ledge where they had landed, lay a seemingly bottomless blackness. They were trapped in a giant coffin of ice. "Only an *idiot* would tell me to relax!"

Ty winced at the word *idiot* but didn't back off. "Look, I know how much it hurts," he said. "I can make the pain go away. Trust me."

Cat's laugh was chopped and cruel, her voice low but full of pain-fueled fury. "You stole my dad's ashes. How could I possibly trust you? I'm going to do what I should have done twice already: call nine-one-one."

Ty started to protest. "But you can't—"

"SHUT UP!" Cat shrieked.

Ty's eyebrows arched, but he said nothing.

Cat struggled onto her side. Pain pulsed through her knee, a drumbeat of misery. She moaned but took a deep breath, then gingerly fished her cell phone from her pocket and flipped it open. The display sent out an eerie glow. She dialed 9-1-1. Immediately the phone beeped and a message appeared: NO SERVICE.

For an instant of unbridled wrath, Cat came within an inch of hurling her phone against the ice. Of course there was no service. They were inside a glacier!

She gritted her teeth and tried to think. Maybe a different server could connect. All they needed were a couple of bars, or maybe even just one to text. "Try yours," she ordered Ty.

He nodded, shed his pack, checked the top pouch, then opened the main compartment. Climbing rope and Uncle Scott's ice axes spilled out before he stopped short and slapped himself on the forehead. "Oh no, it's at home."

Cat gaped, dumbfounded. *"You left your cell phone in Seattle?"*

Ty held up his hands in surrender. "I know, I know. Who goes anywhere without their cell phone? I was so excited about coming here that . . . well, I *thought* I had it with me. It must still be on the kitchen counter."

"Where it does us *absolutely* no good!" Cat snapped. Another spasm shot through her knee. She bowed her head under the intensity of it. How could anything possibly hurt this much?

"C'mon, Cat, let me help you," Ty said. He laid his hand on her shoulder.

With a violent jerk Cat shrugged it off. *"Go away!"* she shouted, and now there was hate in her voice.

It struck home. Like a ruptured tire, Ty slowly sank back onto his heels. Silence fell, broken only by the drip of meltwater off the crevasse walls and Mugs's nervous panting from above.

Until the glacier shifted and let out a sudden snap that crackled through the ice. Ty flinched at the sound. "Whoa!" he said. "This berg talks like its alive or—" He stopped midsentence, a look of sheer horror on his face. "WHAT IS THAT?" he screeched, pointing over Cat's shoulder into the darkness.

Cat startled, and turned to see.

"Made you look!" Ty blurted out, and, in one swift motion, grabbed her by the ankle and heaved backward hard, throwing all of his weight into it.

Cat's knee exploded in agony. There was a grinding pop. She howled and lunged at Ty, lashing out blindly with her fist . . . just as she realized that the pain was miraculously fading.

CHAPTER 12

A REAL CLIFF-HANGER

At first Cat didn't believe it. How could torment so intense evaporate so quickly? Gingerly she tested the mobility of her knee. To her amazement she could move it with only a dull ache to pay. Phew! She closed her phone and slipped it back in her pocket, then brushed the snow from her pants and jacket. Out of the corner of her eye, she snuck a quick glance to see if Ty was gloating with an I-told-you-I-could-fix-it smirk. That's when she realized that he was slumped against the crevasse wall. He wasn't moving.

"Ty?"

Cat knew she'd hit him, clobbered him, really. Who, in her place, wouldn't have? He'd invaded her privacy, stolen her dad's ashes and her dog, fled the scene of multiple crimes, and *then* ambushed her knee. It could be argued quite logically that he deserved to get thumped.

True, he had helped dig her out of the avalanche. But she

wouldn't have gotten caught in the avalanche in the first place if she'd been home where she belonged. She'd had every right to be angry.

Still, she wasn't a violent person. She hadn't meant to whack him, especially that hard. It had been more a reflexive action, like when they were seven and he'd sprung out of the closet. She'd slapped him so hard, his nose had bled. She must have really connected this time, too. Now that she thought about it, her right hand was throbbing as if she'd slammed it into a wall. Had she hit him in the head?

"Hey, Ty?"

Still no movement.

From the lip of the crevasse, Mugs let out a nervous whimper. A spark of alarm flickered in Cat's stomach, then flared to life. She swallowed hard and leaned close to her cousin. There was blood at the corner of his mouth, a bruise blossoming beside his eye.

"Ty?" Was he . . . was he breathing? In the gloom of the crevasse, she couldn't tell. The only sounds were those of her own quick, shallow gulps of air and a distant creak in the glacier, like a door in a haunted house.

Alarm turned quickly to creeping dread. Cat laid trembling fingers on Ty's wrist, desperate to feel a pulse. *Please* let there be a pulse.

Her own heart was pounding so hard, she couldn't detect any beat of his.

Sirens screamed in Cat's head. She pushed herself to her feet, ignoring the ache in her knee. "It was an accident," she pleaded. "I didn't mean to hit you! Really! Hang on, I'll climb out and . . ."

And what? She couldn't think.

Which only fed her growing panic. "I'll climb out and call for help! I was getting two bars earlier up on Backbone Spur. There'll be a signal on the surface of the glacier, too. Really! Hang on! Don't do anything stupid like d—"

The word *die* caught in Cat's throat. She swallowed hard and forced it down. Get going! she ordered herself. Now! Frantically she looked around for her father's ice ax, then remembered— she'd lost it in the avalanche. How was she going to climb up twenty feet of vertical wall if she had no—

Uncle Scott's axes! They were made specifically for climbing steep ice. Cat whirled and scooped them up from where Ty had dumped them out of his pack when looking for his phone. Gripping one ax in each hand, she took a wild, two-arm swing at the crevasse wall. Both picks deflected, sending a shower of ice flakes flying.

From above, Mugs barked.

"Don't worry, Mugs!" Cat called up to him, worry raging through every cell of her body. To herself she screamed, Think! Dad hadn't gotten to ice climbing instruction with her. That was to come when she turned thirteen. But she'd read tons about it in his mountaineering books. She'd studied photos, too, and watched videos.

Text and images flew through Cat's mind. First it was important to set the picks deep so they'd hold. She took another swing at the ice with one of the axes, this time harder.

The pick deflected for a second time.

"Come on!" she begged. She took aim again, making doubly sure to keep the pick steady and true, and drove it at the ice as hard as she could. This time it sank deep, with a solid thunk. A burst of elation. Success! Quickly she did the same with the other.

Now the feet, she reminded herself. She lifted her left foot and poked the front points of her crampons at the crevasse wall. They skated off. She reared back and kicked harder. This time they stuck, but at a price—her knee throbbed.

Cat took a deep breath and hoisted herself up off the ice shelf. The pressure on her forearms and the back of her left calf was immediate. Quickly she set the front points of her right foot— lifting her a total of eighteen inches off the deck—and froze.

What was she doing? She wasn't roped in! There was no one to belay her! She was free soloing, and the books made it *very* clear that there was no margin of error in free soloing. One mistake and she'd peel off the ice.

Peel off the ice and she'd plummet.

Plummet and she'd end up wedged into the bottom of this crevasse like a cork in a bottle.

In minutes the heat from her body would mold the ice to her, freezing her clothes to it. She'd die a slow, miserable death of hypothermia.

Then the crevasse would close up over her, and the glacier would grind her up and spit her out at the base two centuries from now.

That is, if the fall alone didn't kill her.

Cat blinked hard in an attempt to shake off the image and the accompanying fear. Dad had said climbing was at least three-quarters mental. Lose confidence and she'd lose the mental game. Lose the mental game and she was doomed.

Just climb! she ordered herself. Now!

And whatever you do, don't look down.

Cat yanked her left ice ax free and swung it hard and high. It drove into the ice above her with a reassuring thunk. Both axes soon planted, she moved her right foot higher, setting the front points of her crampons solidly. She pulled herself up with the three good points of contact, and kicked her left foot in, then started the process again.

Climb! she kept saying to herself. Climb!

A rhythm quickly developed, axes and front points going. Swing, thunk, swing, thunk, kick, kick. Swing, thunk, swing, thunk, kick, kick.

"Good," Cat said, aloud now. "Just focus on what's right in front of you and keep moving. And whatever you do, DON'T LOOK DOWN!"

In mental control again, Cat attacked the ice, racing for the top as fast as her arms and legs would carry her. Swing, thunk, swing, thunk, kick, kick. Swing, thunk, swing, thunk, kick, kick. Almost there!

She pulled her right ax and looked up to take the next swing, but stopped.

"What?"

It took a moment for the reality of the situation to sink in. Although a six-foot section of the snow bridge had collapsed when she and Ty had fallen through, part of it near the crevasse wall still remained, creating an overhanging roof that blocked her way out. Mugs was pacing back and forth on that precarious lip, his leash dangling down toward her.

"Mugs, get back!" Cat ordered.

Mugs whimpered, the plaintive sound echoing in the crevasse.

"Now!" Cat ordered. "Back!"

To Cat's amazement, Mugs actually backed away.

"Good dog!" she said, but there was anguish in her voice. Lactic acid was building up fast in her forearm and legs. Her muscles screamed in protest. She could feel her grip on the axes starting to slip. She couldn't hold on much longer. Air came in desperate gasps.

Think! If something blocked the only path, what should she do? What would Dad do? Go around? Not an option. There was only one way—through.

Cat launched a desperate attack, chopping with one of her axes at the overhanging lip of the crevasse. Snow cascaded down on her face and into her collar. She closed her eyes and blindly swung again and again. A large chunk broke loose, crashing down onto her. The impact popped her one fixed ice ax free, and in an instant she was catapulting over backward.

"No!" Cat screamed, and swung wildly with both axes. Miraculously, one pick caught in the ice and held. Cat pendulummed into the crevasse wall. Pain shot through her knee.

As if clearing its throat to swallow her whole, the glacier groaned.

Cat looked down. Bad idea. At the sight of the gaping abyss below her, her brain went haywire. Her mind screamed a lunatic dance in her skull, then shut completely down. Pure adrenaline took over as she flailed at the crevasse wall. Finally she stuck the free ax, then one foot, then the other. All points back in contact, she lunged wildly, desperately upward . . . and the next thing she knew, she was sprawled on the surface of the glacier.

Where she was immediately covered with big, wet doggy kisses.

CHAPTER 13

9-1-1

Cat rolled onto her back; breath coming in harsh, rasping gulps; spent to the point of nausea.

And so at first didn't catch the sound echoing up out of the crevasse. At last it registered, and Cat realized that it was applause.

"Bravo." The voice was weak and tenuous, but there was no mistaking it.

"Ty!" Cat crawled over to the lip of the crevasse and peered down through the hole in the snow bridge. Ty looked up at her with a woozy expression on his face. "You're alive!"

Ty winced. "Um . . . yeah, I think so." He put his hand to his head. "Ouch. What happened?"

Cat's face went hot with guilt. "Um . . . well, I kinda . . . hit you."

"Kinda?"

"Well, no, really hit you." She cringed. "Knocked you out. I think I gave you a concussion. Sorry."

Ty touched his mouth and came away with blood on his fingertips. "Whoa, I'm . . . hurt." He looked around with obvious confusion. "How did I—Man, I don't feel so good. . . ."

Cat jumped into action. From her readings on wilderness first aid, she knew that concussions could be dangerous. Ty needed medical care as soon as possible. She sat back and fumbled with cold fingers to get her cell phone from her pocket. "Hold on!" she shouted. "I'll call nine-one-one. We'll get you out of there in no time." To herself she whispered, "If there is reception. *Please* let there be reception!"

She flipped the phone open. "Two bars! Just like up on Backbone Spur!"

"Cat?" Ty called up from below.

She looked back down at her cousin. "Yes."

"While you've got nine-one-one on the phone . . ." He sighed, and for a moment seemed to forget what he was doing. "Oh, yeah, how about ordering me some Mountain Dew? It's an emergency, really."

Cat almost smiled. Despite everything, she had to admit, Ty was gutsy. How many people could keep a sense of humor in a situation like this? She couldn't, she knew. She dialed. "Nine-one-one, done!" she said, announcing the numbers to reassure him. She lifted the phone to her ear. "Ringing, ringing, ringing. Yes! It's ringing, ringing, ringing!"

She was already imagining the rescue: the *thwock-thwock-*

thwock of the helicopter rotors; the backwash of wind as it landed on the glacier; the Storm Mountain Search and Rescue members, whom her father and uncle had loved so much, hauling Ty swiftly and efficiently to safety. Yes, on the anniversary of their fathers' deaths, this ending would be a happy one. They were as good as saved!

A soft click and then a woman's voice. "This is nine-one-one. What is your emergency?"

Words tumbled from Cat's mouth. "My name is Cat Taylor, and my emergency is that my cousin Ty is in a crevasse and he's hurt and—"

Cat stopped, took the phone from her ear, and frowned at it. "Hello? Hey, *hello*? Anybody there? Nine-one-one? Please! Don't . . ."

She trailed off into silence. Her phone was dead.

CHAPTER 14

PLAN E

"What's wrong?" Ty said. "They out of Mountain Dew?"

Cat stared at her phone in disbelief. "I had them, a good, clear signal. Then it just stopped working."

Ty looked up at her for a moment, blinking. "When's the last time you charged it?"

Now Cat bristled. What did he mean, when was the last time she charged it? She *always* charged her cell phone, every night without fail. It was part of the unbroken routine: floss and brush teeth, set the alarm, put a glass of water on the bedside table, plug her phone into—

Uh-oh. Realization hit Cat like a brick. She'd been so wrapped up in Ty's surprise visit last night that she'd completely spaced out recharging her phone. "Oh no," she groaned. "We're doomed."

"Naw," Ty said, the word slurring on his tongue. "There are worse things in life, you know." He flashed a loopy grin up at her.

"Like shopping for appliances with your mom? You ever done that? It's worse. Definitely."

He giggled like a drunk at his own joke. "But anyway, okay, so Plan A to call nine-one-one didn't work. Haven't you ever heard of Plan B? There's *always* a Plan B." He hesitated for a moment with a dazed expression on his face. "What is it?"

Cat shrugged listlessly. She hadn't thought beyond calling for help. All her hope had been wrapped up in it. She hugged Mugs to her. He leaned into her embrace and looked up at her with adoring eyes. "I don't know what to do," she said.

"Well then, forget Plan B," Ty said. "How about Plan C? Plan C, as in . . ." He trailed off for a moment, then brightened. "As in Ty climbs out of here just like you did. Plan C for *climb*. Yeah!"

He grabbed his pack and began rummaging around in the main compartment. His brow quickly knitted with concern. "Where are my dad's ice tools? I'm sure they were in here before. Did you—" He looked up at Cat. "Did you swipe 'em?"

"I needed to climb out," Cat said.

A dopey smile lifted one side of Ty's mouth. "Oh yeah, so you could call nine-one-one. Do you have good reception? Have you called yet?"

Cat started to remind Ty that yes, she'd called just a moment ago, but stopped herself. Clearly, he was not making sense. Not making sense because she'd whacked him in the head and given him a concussion.

A renewed wave of guilt reared its ugly head, and for a second Cat felt herself starting to sink under its harsh stare.

In the meantime, Ty had struggled to his feet. "Oh well," he said, "who needs ice axes?" He staggered and almost pitched headfirst off the ledge.

"Whoa!" he said. "Steady, dude." He ran his hands along the crevasse wall, found a fracture in the ice, and started trying to climb up, as if it were rock.

Cat jolted back to life. "Ty, stop!" she yelled down at him. "You can't climb up here with—"

"You really shouldn't tell someone they can't do something," Ty said, "when they already are."

He wedged a crampon into the crack in the ice and pulled weakly, attempting to hoist himself upward. His foot slipped, and he slid back down onto the ice shelf.

"Ty," Cat said. "Really, that is *not* going to work."

Ty shook his head. "We've been through this before. Repetition is boring. Either I have already succeeded, or I'm about to."

Mugs nudged Cat's hand with his nose. Cat clutched him to her. "Ty," she said, more insistent now. "Don't. Please. Let's think of another Plan C." Should she lower his dad's ice axes to him and then belay him out? No, he was too weak, and his mind was muddled. "Just wait a minute and let me think, would you?"

"Borrrring!" Ty sang. "I can't hearrrr you!"

"But—"

"No buts about it, Ms. Butthead." He doggedly stuck his hand back in the crack in the ice.

Any other time and place and Cat would have snipped at

him. No need to start calling names like he did when they were kids! Ms. Butthead? Couldn't he do any better than that?

But not this time and place. "Ty," Cat pleaded.

Ty ignored her and kept trying.

"Ty."

Trying.

"Ty, listen to me!"

Still trying.

"Ty! Stop acting like a five-year-old!"

Ty let out a groan and plunked back down on the ice shelf. He rubbed his head. "You know what?" he said. "On second thought, I don't think I'm going to be able to climb out right now. I'm off my game. You know what I mean? It's time for Plan . . . What would it be? Oh, yeah, Plan A, B, C, *D*! You know what that stands for?"

"No."

"*Down*," Ty said. "As in: You and Mugs hike *down* to the house and call nine-one-one on the landline."

Cat startled. "You want me to leave you?"

Ty nodded. "Yep. Take Mugs and go. I'll just hang out here in this lovely crevasse until help comes. You seem to really like logical things. Well, this is logical, right?"

Cat considered Ty's point. If she hiked down, it would take her at least an hour and a half to reach her house, then that much longer for Search and Rescue to get mobilized and make it up here.

If they could make it up here at all. She glanced back over her shoulder at the sky. Clouds were getting thicker by the minute and lowering fast. The dragon was closing in.

Ty wanted logic? The logic was as clear as it was inarguable. They simply didn't have time for her to go get help.

So Plan D was out. It was Plan E's turn. Plan E for *emergency*. Cat had no choice. It was up to her to pull off this rescue.

CHAPTER 15

SIX-TO-ONE ODDS

Ty argued at first. "Really, you should go for help." But not with much heart. When Cat told him to save it for someone who was actually listening, he caved in quickly. "Okay then," he said, "throw me a rope and haul me out."

If only it were that simple. Cat knew that there was no way she alone could just lower a rope and pull Ty straight up twenty feet of vertical ice. Between the load of his body and the friction on the rope as it slid over the lip of the crevasse, it would take an Olympic weight lifter to muscle him to the surface. Actually, a superhero was more like it.

Being a mere mortal, she would have to put physics to use and build a pulley system to create a mechanical advantage. If done right, she could literally hoist a pickup truck out of the crevasse by herself.

Of course, this was easier conceived than done. Theory was one thing, practice another. Building a pulley system required

know-how, of which she had a lot; she could talk crevasse rescue systems like a pro mountain guide. However, it also required
experience, another thing Dad had promised to provide when
Cat turned thirteen.

True, there was that one time she had used shoestrings to
rig a model of a simple Z-pulley with a three-to-one mechanical
advantage on top of her desk. She'd easily hoisted her stapler a
few inches off the bedroom floor. But before today she'd never
even peered down into a crevasse, much less built a system that
could actually haul a real live human being out of one. If what
she built didn't work, he'd be stuck and in big trouble. If what
she built suddenly failed, as in ripped from the ice, Ty would
fall, probably to his death. Everything depended on Cat getting
it right.

The glacier let out another groan, then a pop that made Cat
jump. She imagined the entire wall of the crevasse suddenly giving way, falling down on Ty, crushing him like Mugs Stump had
been crushed on Denali. She shuddered at the thought, closed her
eyes, and curled forward under the weight of so much responsi-
bility. If only Dad were here . . .

"Hey, you okay?"

Cat looked down into Ty's questioning face. "Yeah," she lied,
forcing as much optimism into her voice as possible. "This will
take a few minutes, though. I've got to put in an anchor and—"

"An *anchor*? You brought an anchor up here?"

Cat faked a laugh and rolled her eyes. "Not a boat anchor,
dummy, a *climbing* anchor that I'll build out of ice screws, and

slings made of webbing, and carabiners, too—you can never have too many carabiners—and then . . . oh, just wait until you get up here and you'll see."

If she could get him up there. Would a three-to-one mechanical advantage be enough? The more she thought about it, the more she thought not. She'd read about a new five-to-one hauling system in one of the climbing magazines. How did that system go? She'd cut the article out and dropped it in the file marked CREVASSE RESCUE. If only she had it with her!

Cat rolled her eyes again, but this time at herself. So now she was going to start packing magazine articles? What was next, books and DVDs? And don't forget the laptop. Never know when she'd need to do some research. Might as well bring the filing cabinet, too!

She shook her head at the absurdity of the idea. No, she was on her own. Memory would have to do. Seems there was a six-to-one that could be rigged straight off the Z-pulley. But did she have enough rope? Better get down to business. She'd figure it out as she went . . . hopefully.

Cat moved away from the lip of the crevasse, unshouldered her pack, and flipped the top pouch back to find herself face-to-face with the urn containing her father's ashes. A hollow feeling threatened the pit of her stomach, but she fought it off. *Think!* she reminded herself for what seemed like the hundredth time that day. *Stay focused!*

Careful to avoid touching the urn, she reached around it and pulled out a small mountain of her father's gear. She began sorting. From what she'd read, she knew she needed two ice screws to anchor the pulley system to the surface of the glacier.

No, four. She should back up each screw in case one pulled out. Redundancy was the key to safety. She started to work, clearing away loose snow. Once she hit solid ice, she began twisting the first screw into place, but then stopped.

Should the shaft go straight in or at an angle? She couldn't remember. And, come to think of it, once the screws were in place, should she tie off the slings and pre-equalize the pressure or make the anchor self-equalizing? How, exactly, did you do either?

As if he could read her mind, Ty called from below. "You sure this will pull me up? Maybe I need to go on a quick diet." He laughed. "I've been eating too many bean burritos with extra cheese. But who could blame me? Best food in the world, you know."

Cat went back to work on the ice screw. She was having trouble getting the teeth at the end to grab. She cranked it extra hard, and it fell over. Anxiety rose like angry bees in her head. Still, she managed to lob a volley back at Ty. "The best food in the world is homemade pesto pizza!"

"No way!" Ty shouted back. "Burritos!"

Cat gave the screw another hard twist and finally got the threads engaged. Cranking the handle furiously, she quickly twisted it in tight. Now for number two . . .

Mugs inched over to the lip of the crevasse and peered down.

From below, Ty yelled, "Get back, Mugs!"

"Yeah, get back!" Cat said, then, without thinking, added, "Do what Ty says."

"That's right!" Ty said gleefully. "*Everyone* should do what Ty says!"

Cat frowned. Ty seemed to be rapidly getting over the knock on the head and returning to his old frustrating self. "Please come here, Mugsy," she begged.

Mugs whined, then barked down at Ty, but finally obeyed and moved away from the crevasse edge. She quickly tied the practice-rope leash to her with a figure-eight follow-through, then went back to work building her anchor.

Compared to the first screw, the next three went in fairly easily. Cat clipped locking carabiners and slings to them to form the backup, then created a master point with a longer sling, careful to twist one loop. The anchor was done.

From below, Cat could hear Ty talking to himself. "Man, it's cold down here. And dark, too. Where's my headlamp? Oh yeah, here. . . . Let there be light! Whoa! This place is awesome—beautiful when you stop and take a look."

Cat imagined him sitting on the ice ledge, gazing around at the interior of the crevasse as if it were Disneyland.

"Yeah, man, incredible shade of blue! It's like it's electric or something. And the water dripping down the sides. It glistens. Cool, huh?"

Cool wasn't the word that came to Cat's mind. She turned her attention to rigging the actual pulley system. Let's see, the rope had to go through the master point, then loop back on itself. A sling and a carabiner attached with a Prusik knot would complete the three-to-one advantage. To make it six-to-one, she would have to—

"Hey, Cat?" Ty said.

Cat let out a sigh. "What?"

"Do you believe in luck?"

Cat didn't answer. She didn't have time to think about luck. How did that six-to-one go?

"I do," Ty said. "I put my right sock on first every morning for good luck." He was silent for a moment. "I can roll my tongue. Want to see?"

Cat flared. "Yeah, why don't you come on up here and show me!" Couldn't he tell she was trying to concentrate? There would have to be a ratchet for the pulley, too, so Ty didn't slip back down while she was advancing the Prusik.

"Gotcha," Ty said. "I'll see what I can do."

"Great," Cat said, sarcasm dripping, and focused again on the pulley.

By the time she finally had the rescue system laid out and ready, at least twenty minutes had passed and Cat was teetering on the edge of losing it. Her knee throbbed. Her head swam with information she'd read but never applied. Freezing rain was beginning to tick her jacket.

She took a deep breath. "Okay," she called to Ty. She eased back over to the lip of the crevasse. "I'll toss you the rope and—"

She looked down to find the ice shelf empty. Ty was nowhere to be seen.

"Ty?" Alarm rocketed through Cat's body. Had he fallen in? "TY!"

"See, I really can curl my tongue."

Cat shrieked and jumped at the voice that came from behind her. She spun to find Ty standing on the surface of the glacier, his tongue stuck out and rolled into a perfect tube.

CHAPTER 16

FIGURE-EIGHT FOLLOW-THROUGH

Cat went from shock to fury in a heartbeat. "WHAT ARE YOU DOING HERE?"

Ty's grin dropped. "Well, you said to come show you that I could curl my tongue. I thought—"

"But *how* did you get up here? You were trapped in the crevasse!"

Ty pointed to a hole in the glacier twenty yards away. "With my headlamp on, I could see that the ledge we'd fallen onto kept going. I followed it, and it started angling up, kind of like an exit ramp on the freeway. So I kept motoring until I was right under the roof of snow. I just punched my way through. And here I am!"

Cat glared.

"I didn't mean to scare you," Ty said.

"You didn't scare me!" Cat snapped.

Ty's eyebrows went up, but then he shrugged and changed

the subject. "Cool thing-a-ma-doohicky," he said, pointing at Cat's pulley system. "No doubt it would have worked great."

Despite everything, Cat felt herself soften at the compliment.

"If we had, like, actually needed it," Ty added.

Cat stiffened again. Ty, it was clear, had no clue of his effect on people, and never would. "We'd better get moving," she said. The freezing rain was turning to snow, the wind gusting stronger by the minute. She pulled up her jacket hood.

Mugs wagged his tail and whined. "It's okay, Mugsy," Cat said, as if it were true. She began to dismantle the pulley system and coil the rope.

Ty joined in, but then stopped with an ice screw dangling from one finger. "Hey, Cat, with all of the hidden crevasses, shouldn't we be tied together?"

Cat started to ask just where—since he'd never taken his dad up on learning anything about mountaineering—he'd picked up this sage advice. At the skateboard park? But then she realized that he was right.

Which galled her to no end.

Still, she acted as if this were a no-brainer that she'd been thinking of all along. "Of course we rope up. You always rope up when on a glacier. Get your harness on."

"Gotcha," Ty said, and unshouldered his pack.

Cat quickly slipped into her harness and cinched it tight, then, with the fingers of experience, tied a figure-eight follow-through onto the belay loop. She was set to go.

Ty, on the other hand, was still rummaging around in his pack. Finally he pulled out his harness but got the leg loops tangled and the waist belt twisted. "Whoa," he said. "What planet did this thing come from?"

It took Cat at least five minutes to talk him through putting it on, especially the critical part about doubling back the waist belt to secure it. She threw him the other end of the rope. "Okay, so tie in to your belay loop and let's get going," she said, frustration growing.

Ty looked at the rope, then his harness, and then up at Cat, and she knew he didn't even know what a belay loop was, much less how to tie a figure-eight follow-through onto one. She tied it for him. He studied the knot for a minute, then said, "Oh, why didn't you say so?"

Cat just shook her head. She was now roped to a thief—not to mention a smart aleck—by a slender thread of eight-millimeter rope. Implicit in the act was the fact that their fates were now literally linked. Better to not think about that . . .

Cat handed Ty one of the two remaining ice axes. "If I drop through another snow bridge or slip on the climb back up the moraine, throw yourself on the ice and dig the ax pick in, and brace yourself for the jolt. You've got to be ready. I'll be depending on you."

"Will do," Ty said. "We're a team now, aren't we, just like the good old days!"

Cat considered the thought. She had a gimped-up knee and he'd had his marbles knocked loose, but yes, she had to admit that they were a team. Whether or not it was "just like the good old days" was open to debate.

"Pay attention, teammate," she said. "Please."

Ty grinned and mimed tipping his hat. "No worries, ma'am," he said in a deep cowboy baritone. "Let's get this doggy drive going. Hee-yah! Giddyup, Mugsy!"

Cat rolled her eyes but said nothing. Snow was falling steadily now. She led the way across the glacier, careful to stay as far as possible from any depression that could be hiding a crevasse. Once, two trenches of sagging snow converged, and the threesome had to backtrack and go around. Then not more than twenty steps later, Cat had a strong and unpleasant sense that they were in danger. She poked the shaft of her ice ax into the surface in front of her, and it went straight through. She jumped back, and they gave the hidden crevasse a wide berth.

After what seemed like forever, they finally stepped off the glacier onto solid ground. Cat surveyed the steep slope of Backbone Spur looming above them. Through the swirling snow she could just make out the wind-sculpted cornices lined up along its crest. "Hang fire" her dad had called it, due to the danger of it breaking off and roaring down onto climbers. Better to take the path cleared by the avalanche, she thought. It was on the most precipitous part of the slope, but at least the cornice at the top was gone. She'd seen to that earlier.

"Okay, up we go," Cat said. "I'll kick steps and you follow. Remember to use your ax. You ready?"

Ty nodded from under his hood.

Halfway up, the grade turned from hard-packed snow to blue ice. Cat's crampons began to bounce off, and she had to swing her feet with even more power, which sent a pulse of pain through her knee with every kick. Still, her only real purchase was with the front points of her crampons. Mugs was having problems with traction, too, his toenails scritching on the ice.

"Careful here," Cat cautioned.

"No worries," Ty said, just as his crampons slipped and his feet whipped out from under him.

CHAPTER 17

THERE'S NO PLACE LIKE HOME

Cat threw herself onto the slope. She stabbed her ax pick at the ice, bore down with all her might, and waited for the jolt in the rope when the slack ran out. It didn't come.

Mugs whined, splayed spread-eagle on the ice, eyes wide. Heart pounding in her ears, Cat reached out and pulled him to her, then looked over her shoulder at Ty. He had actually arrested his own fall and was already back on his feet, looking dazed but moving up toward her.

"Wait!' Cat said. "Give me a second to get situated to belay you." She sat up and began to frantically reel rope in. "Wait!" she repeated, but Ty kept coming. "Really!" Cat insisted. "There's too much slack. If you slip again, this time I'm not—"

Ty took another step and his foot skated off the icy slope. He went down face-first and started to slide. Instinctively, Cat grabbed the rope. Ty caught a crampon and flipped over backward, tumbling completely out of control. He reached the end of the rope. It yanked in Cat's hands, zipping across her palms, sending fire through her thin gloves and into her flesh.

Cat cried out, but dug in her heels and held on until everything stopped. "I said *wait*!" she shouted. "And I meant it. Stay right where you are until I get situated."

Mugs barked twice, as if to say, "Sit. Stay."

"Sorry," Ty said. He was grinning, but a mix of fear and pain showed on the edges. He waited until Cat moved off the glare ice onto softer snow. She kicked out a small level spot to sit and wrapped the rope around her body for a sitting belay—the quick, simple method Dad had showed her how to use in a pinch. She gave the signal for Ty to move upward again.

Cat brought in slack as Ty carefully made his way back over the icy spot. It was snowing full-on now. Storm Mountain was once again living up to its reputation. Cat kept hauling in rope.

When he was at her side, Ty sat down. "Thanks," he said. "You saved my butt." He raised a hand to give her a high five.

Cat weakly raised a hand to meet it. Ty stopped short. "Whoa!" he said, concern in his eyes. "You're shaking like crazy!"

Cat stared at her trembling hand and realized she was shivering all over. Ty was, too, she now saw, chilled from his time in the crevasse. She looked back up over her shoulder at the crest of Backbone Spur. Clouds boiled over the cornices and raced down toward them. The temperature must have dropped twenty degrees in the last ten minutes. The dragon was on the hunt. Cat could feel its predatory eyes on them. For a moment the day's collective chaos—the chase after Ty, the avalanche, the crevasse fall and escape, the deteriorating weather—nearly overwhelmed her. She felt like giving up.

And what? Die right there, out in the open? Cat shook her head. "We've got to keep moving," she said, as much to herself as to Ty. She pushed herself to her feet. "Let's go. Stay sharp."

Thankfully, the steepness of the slope lessened right above them. Cat plodded upward. If they could just get to the top of the ridge, they'd be home free. She quickened her pace, tugging Ty toward the crest of Backbone Spur. Twenty more feet. Almost there, and they'd be able to see the Hallelujah Gate and get oriented. In an hour or so she'd be walking through the front door of her house.

A sudden wave of nostalgia swept over Cat. It would so good to see Mom again. Home, home, there really was no place like home. Cat sank the pick of her ice ax into the snow and used it to pull herself up the slope. "There's no place like home," she chanted beneath each breath. "There's no place like home." She powered upward, towing Ty and Mugs behind her.

"Yes!" Cat yelled as she finally topped Backbone Spur. Only to be slammed full in the face by a wall of wind-driven snow.

CHAPTER 18

A CHAOS OF WHITE

Cat staggered back, arm raised to shield her face from the storm's onslaught. A gust buffeted her, almost knocking her over. Snow rose up off the ridge crest, corkscrewing into wild white tornadoes. The lee side of the ridge had offered shelter from the brunt of the blizzard. Here its power was tenfold.

Mugs whined.

"It's okay, Mugsy," Cat shouted, only to hear her words shredded by the wind.

Ty struggled up beside her. The expression on his face was dull and pallid, but he forced a smile. "Great day for a hike, huh? What a view!"

Cat peered down the mountain, hoping for a break in the clouds, a glimpse of the Hallelujah Gate. Find it and she'd located the beacon pointing the way home. Snow swirled violently before her eyes. She could barely tell where earth ended and sky began.

The world was quickly beginning to look like the inside of a Ping-Pong ball. She could see ten feet, maybe.

"Yeah, absolutely perfect day for a hike," she yelled, trying to sound jovial, trying to ignore the dread churning in her gut. This was quickly becoming a whiteout. "Let's shorten the rope between us, so we can be sure to see each other." She tied the rope off and coiled the extra over her shoulder into a Kiwi coil. "Ready?" she said.

"Lead on," Ty answered.

At first Cat followed the crest of Backbone Spur, hoping to spot tracks. Find any set—hers, Ty's, even Mugs's—and it would be like following bread crumbs to the bakery.

It quickly became apparent, however, that all of their tracks had been filled in by blowing snow. Afraid of another cornice breaking off and catching them in an avalanche, Cat lead Mugs and Ty off the ridge crest and onto the broad, open slope of the mountain.

The wind rose to a shriek. Visibility dropped to near zero. The effect made Cat's head spin. She couldn't tell up from down. She stopped, dizzy, disoriented.

"What?" Ty called from behind. He came up beside her. Mugs whined again. Ty reached down and patted Mugs's head to reassure him. "Which way?"

Which way, indeed. Cat threw her pack onto the snow and opened the top pouch. That was where she kept her dad's compass.

Mugs nosed in, no doubt hoping for food. Cat could sympathize. Her stomach was a hollow, crying pit.

But now was not the time. "Back, Mugs," she ordered. She fetched the compass, opened it, only to realize that it was worthless if she couldn't see to take bearings off landmarks and intersect the lines to triangulate their location.

Ty was on his knees now, looking into Cat's pack. "Here's a map!" he said, and pulled Cat's topographic map of Storm Mountain out into the open. He unfolded it just as a great blast of wind hit them, ripping it from his hands. It sailed off, and was gone.

Ty's face crumpled. "Aw, man, I'm sorry!"

Anger flashed through Cat, but quickly faded. "It doesn't matter," she said. And it was true. "A map isn't much good if you don't know where you are on it."

Ty forced a wan smile. "Can't we just head straight down? We're bound to run into the tree line, right? And then your house, right?"

Cat considered the idea. In theory, yes, down was the right direction. But at what angle? Should they bear east a bit? Thinking back, it seemed to Cat that she'd climbed slightly west on the way up.

Or had she? Maybe she'd borne more southwest. At the time she was so upset and intent on catching Ty that she really hadn't paid much attention to what she was doing. She'd just done it.

Now she was confused about which way to go. Get it exactly right and they'd be back at the Hallelujah Gate. Trace her track down from there and another hour of descent would land them in her living room, munching on pesto pizza and drinking hot mochas.

If she got the angle of descent right. Guess wrong, off by just a few degrees, and she'd miss the mark completely. With visibility like this, she could walk within ten feet of the Hallelujah Gate and not see it. Not see it and they could end up wandering into the Cloudy River Canyon or walk right off the edge of the Boedon Cliffs. Get it wrong, even just a hair wrong, and they could easily die. The margin of error was minuscule.

Still, they had to try. "This way," Cat said. She got to her feet and helped Ty up. They both lowered their heads and pushed down the slope. The wind blasted them even harder. Snow pelted their faces.

No more than twenty feet later Cat felt a tug on the rope. Thinking it was Mugs resisting walking into the wind, she turned instead to see Ty struggling to his feet. Just as he righted himself, the wind roared and toppled him again. Cat staggered back to where he lay.

"Sorry," he yelled above the howl. "I'm holding you up. Go on down. Get help, then send them back for me."

There it was again, an out, a chance to escape. This time it barely registered on Cat's radar. "We've been through this already," she said. "I'm not leaving you, end of discussion. Got it?"

"But I'm so tired," Ty moaned. "Can't we just rest for a minute?"

Cat had to admit, it sounded good. There was a big part of her that was crying out to curl up in a ball and pretend none of this was happening, close her eyes, and rest. She was so cold, and exhausted, and hungry, and feeling so lost and overwhelmed.

But another part of her brain, the part that had read and cataloged so many climbing stories, knew better. Both she and Ty were exhibiting symptoms of hypothermia. Lie down out in the open like this, exposed to such wind and cold, and they'd never get up again.

Mugs nuzzled Cat's hand, then Ty's.

"Come on, Ty!" Cat urged. She grabbed his arm and pulled. "Get up!"

"Yes, ma'am," Ty said, and saluted. He struggled to his feet, stumbled into Cat, and they both went down.

The wind bellowed. Snow raged across the side of the mountain, pummeling them. The reality of the storm was far beyond anything Cat had ever imagined. Hearing Dad and Uncle Scott talk of struggling against the elements on a big peak was one thing. Being there in the midst of this chaos of white was another. She fought back panic and told herself to breathe. She ducked her head and tried to calm her thoughts. What would Dad have done?

The answer was as simple as it was horrible: Cat had escaped the clutches of the snow twice—from the avalanche and then from the crevasse—but now she and Mugs and Ty had to seek its shelter.

"We've got to dig in," Cat yelled.

Ty's look of confusion said it all. "What?"

"We've got to get out of this weather," Cat shouted above the roaring wind. "We need to build a snow cave and wait out the storm."

Ty's brow knitted. "But a snow cave is where our dads—

"I know, I know," Cat said. A snow cave was where their fathers had died. "This will be different, though," she insisted. "We'll make it."

She hoped. Oh Lord, did she hope.

CHAPTER 19

JUST IN CASE

Unfortunately, despite all the reading that Cat had done, there had always been one subject she had avoided—how to build a snow cave. Just the thought of it brought up images of her father and Uncle Scott digging in on that small ledge on the North Face Direct. She had always turned the page.

Now she wished she'd faced the discomfort and read on. The combination of skills her dad had taught her and her book knowledge had helped her get out of the crevasse and rig a pulley system that would probably have worked if she'd been given the chance. But now she had nothing to fall back on.

The wind shrieked across the mountain. Cat's jacket flapped under the force of it, cracking in guttural tones. She could feel it vibrating her body. Don't think about Dad, she told herself. Concentrate on the task at hand. First thing, logically, was to get out of the wind on the lee side of . . . something . . . anything . . .

She spotted a small swale. "C'mon!" she yelled at Ty. "Over here!"

They staggered into the depression and found themselves thigh-deep in windblown snow. Cat untied both herself and her cousin from the rope and gave Ty the leash to hold on to Mugs. She then threw her pack down and got out her snow shovel. It seemed to take forever to fix the telescoping handle to the blade, but finally it clicked into place. She began digging straight down into the drift.

Ty started to help, scooping out snow with his hands.

"You got a shovel?" Cat shouted over the wind.

Ty shook his head. "I left it in Seattle to make room for my dad's ashes. Bad idea, huh?" He flung snow through his legs and out behind him like a dog.

Mugs joined in, as if he knew. The dull throb in Cat's knee grew to a pounding pain. She gritted her teeth. "Good boy, Mugs," she said. "Dig! Dig!"

They all kept excavating, down until they hit a layer of ice so hard it might as well have been rock. Uh-oh. What now?

The wind buffeted them again, hurling snow parallel to the ground. Mugs whined. Cat shielded her face and tried to think through the terror raging inside her. Digging a hole was out, and actually made no sense now that she stopped to consider the situation. Then it came to her. "Burrow sideways!" she said. "Into the drift!"

"Yeah!" Ty said, suddenly full of energy. "Let me dig awhile!" Not waiting for an okay, he grabbed the shovel from Cat and began tunneling feverishly. Without a tool, Cat now resorted to flinging snow out of the way with her hands.

After a few minutes Ty said, "I think that's big enough." He crawled inside and curled back into a corner of the cave, then whistled for Mugs. "Here, big boy!" Mugs zipped inside. "Yep, it's tight, but there's room for all of us! Hey, where you going? Cat, come on in. Get out of the wind."

Cat had backed away, fleeing visions of a small snow cave on the North Face Direct. How could she crawl into a coffin of her own digging?

A savage blast of wind pushed her even farther away from the entrance, as if to say: "Yes, stay out here so the dragon can have you." Cat took a deep breath and crawled in.

Ty blew out a puff of air, which fogged in front of his face. "Welcome to the Storm Mountain Resort!" he proclaimed.

Cat slumped against the snow cave's wall, suddenly all too aware of how cold, wet, and utterly exhausted she was. Her fingers were numb, as well as her brain. She felt as if she'd been beaten with a stick, then run over by a truck.

Ty grinned. "This is just like the forts we used to build back when were kids. Remember? Couch cushions on your living room floor?"

Cat said nothing, just took in their shelter. The space was barely tall enough to sit up in. She was freezing.

Outside, the wind wailed like a banshee. Ty flinched at the sound, then went silent. When, after a moment, he spoke again, his words were somber. "Hey, Cat?"

She fought off a shiver. "Yes."

"I'm thinking that we should write a letter to our moms to explain . . ." He stopped, hesitated for a moment, then shrugged. "Just in case we don't make it. . . . Well, you know, just in case."

CHAPTER 20

WRITING UP A STORM

Outside, the wind gusted to a deafening roar. Cat huddled against the back wall of the cave as a swirl of snow reached in like a dragon's claw. "No," she said, her mouth a thin line of resolve. "We'll make it through this. There's no need to write a letter."

Ty leaned close. "But—"

"No!" Cat pushed him away. She turned her attention to Mugs, as if that would shut Ty up. "Hey, Mugsy." She rubbed her dog's ears just the way he liked.

Mugs closed his eyes and grinned his doggy grin, acting for all the world as if this were a normal day. Talk about living in the moment. It didn't matter to Mugs that they were in a life-or-death situation. Rub his ears and he was one happy snow-cave camper.

Out of the corner of her eye, Cat could see Ty watching her. "I'll do the actual writing," he said. He shivered. "You could just help me figure out what to say."

Cat kept her eyes on her dog. "Wish I had your fur coat,

Mugsy," she said. "I'm cold." She snugged her jacket collar up around her neck.

Ty let out a long, slow sigh. "Well, if that's the way you want it, then I'll write the letter myself." He pulled his pack to him and opened the top pouch. Rummaging around inside, he mumbled to himself. "Yep, I knew I'd tossed in a pen. Always need a pen handy. But did I put in a notebook? No way."

He rifled through the main compartment. "Okay, I guess this will have to do," he said, and pulled a crumpled piece of paper into view. He smoothed it out on his knee, then flipped it over to the unused side. "Looks like I better get it right on the first go. No rewriting, like my usual twenty-three times."

Ty removed his gloves, rubbed his hands together to warm them, then set to work. "Dear Mom," he said, but stopped when no ink appeared on the page. He had to tap the pen point and scribble in the corner of the paper, but finally got the ink flowing. "Dear Mom," he said again, writing as he went. "If you are reading this letter, that means things didn't go so well for Cat and me."

Cat cinched her jacket hood tight. Still, she couldn't block out Ty's voice.

"I know this must be hard," he was saying. "But I—" He scribbled out the pronoun. "But *we* hope you can get over it quickly and—"

"Wait a minute!" Cat interrupted. "My mom still hasn't gotten over *Dad* dying, and that was two whole years ago. There is no way she is going to *quickly* get over me—" A shiver racked her body. "If you're going to do it, then do it right."

Ty eyed her. "I thought you didn't want to write a letter."

"I don't!"

"Well, if you don't want to, then don't tell me how to write it."

Cat scowled. "Yeah, but you're goofing it up."

"Am not."

"Are too."

"Am not."

"Are too."

Ty grinned. "Just like when we were kids. You've got to have the last word."

"Do not," Cat said.

"See?" Ty shot back, jabbing a finger at her. "I told you!"

Cat started to retort, but stopped herself. She cinched her jacket hood even tighter, until there was only a small opening for her eyes.

Ty chuckled. "Well, that's mature looking . . . mature for a preschooler."

Cat turned away. She would not be baited with insults. Talk about acting like a two-year-old . . .

"So where was I?" Ty asked himself, although with plenty of volume so that Cat would be sure to hear. "Oh, yeah, here we— no, here *I* go . . ."

He droned on and on, something about grief and how he couldn't keep it bottled up anymore. At one point, his voice cracked and he wiped away tears.

Cat did her best to push his words, and the idea behind his words, aside, and watched the snow slashing sideways past the cave opening. In her head she counted down from one hundred, and fumed. Why couldn't he at least write quietly?

To her great relief Ty finally ran out of room on his one page. "Done!" he said. "I could have gone on, but it's pretty sweet as it is, if I do say so myself."

Cat hunkered down more, pulled herself into a smaller ball, and said nothing. She could feel Ty's eyes on her.

"Boy, I sure worked up an appetite doing all that writing, though," he said. "You hungry?"

From deep in her jacket, Cat let out an explosive snort. "Of course I'm hungry, you idiot!"

Ty ignored the insult. "How about a burrito?" he asked cheerfully.

Cat opened her hood enough to glare out at him.

Ty returned the glare with a grin. "Burritos are the best food in the world, like I've been telling you." He pulled the greasy brown paper bag from his pack and held it up.

Mugs jumped to attention, his eyes glued on the goodies.

Ty patted him on the head. "Yeah, you know good food when you smell it, don't you, husky dog!" He turned back to Cat. "But for those who have no clue, then how about some pizza?"

"Stop it!" Cat snapped.

Ty raised an eyebrow. He set down the burritos and dug deeper into his pack. "Of course I'm not talking about just any old pizza," he said. Then, with great flare, he pulled a bulging plastic Ziploc bag out and dangled it in front of Cat's face. "I'm talking about homemade *pesto* pizza!"

CHAPTER 21

FOOD FIGHT

"Where did you get that?" Cat demanded.

"The kitchen counter at your house," Ty said. "I thought there was no way you could eat it all by your little lonesome, so—"

"So you just helped yourself!" Cat finished for him, livid at the thought.

Ty shrugged. "Well, yeah."

Mugs nosed closer, eyes darting back and forth between the the sack of burritos and bag full of pizza.

Outside the snow cave, the wind growled. Inside, Cat steamed. First, Ty stole her dad's ashes; then, her dog; and now she finds out he ripped off her homemade pizza to boot! "Give me that!" she barked, and snatched her property back.

Ty seemed unfazed. He reached into his paper bag and fished out a burrito, then unwrapped it. Mugs whined. Ty took a big bite. "Mmmm," he said, "refried beans never tasted so good. Or cheese and tangy salsa. Nice corn tortilla, too."

Cat couldn't believe it. "We're stranded on Storm Mountain in a raging snowstorm, and what do you do? First, write a morbid letter to our moms. Then, you flip and go TV on me, like an ad for Taco Bell. What is *wrong* with you?"

Ty swallowed and smacked his lips. "Nothing is wrong with me. And actually, as I said before, these burritos are not from Taco Bell. They're from Ricardo's in Seattle. Best food in the world!"

"You've got to be kidding," Cat said. "That stuff is nothing but greasy—" She stopped short, bit her tongue. What was she doing arguing about food with a bozo brain when their lives were on the line?

Ty took another bite. He closed his eyes as he chewed, clearly savoring the moment, then swallowed. "I guess you think that your pesto pizza is better," he said.

"Yes!" Cat snapped back. She couldn't help herself. Ty needed to be set straight. To demonstrate her point, she tore the Ziploc bag open and grabbed a slice of pizza. Defiantly, she bit into it and chewed dramatically so Ty would be sure to see how good it was.

Ty shook his head. "No way." He popped the rest of the burrito in his mouth and rubbed his belly in satisfaction as he chewed. "Burritos are the best. And that is a fact."

Cat gave him her best withering look. "No, pesto pizza is better."

"Burritos."

"*Homemade* pesto pizza."

They both glared.

"I know," Ty said. "We'll let Mugs decide."

At the mention of his name, Mugs perked up even more. His tail wagged furiously, swishing snow back and forth.

"Yeah," Ty went on, "let's bet to see which he scarfs down first, and whoever loses has to eat—"

"Stop!" Cat snapped, coming back to her senses. The fact that she'd gotten sucked into Ty's whirlpool of insanity fueled the backlash. "This is crazy. *You* are crazy. I'm cold and wet and we're pinned down in a snow cave by a storm just like the one that killed our fathers! We're in danger! Get it? *Danger!* The last thing on the planet I need is one of your stupid, juvenile games!"

Ty nodded. "Exactly! One of my stupid, juvenile games that will keep your mind off the cold and the wet and the fact that we're pinned down in a snow cave by a storm just like the one that killed our fathers." He grinned. "Just like arguing with me has done so far, hasn't it?"

Cat started to yell no! but then, to her surprise, realized not only that Ty was right—arguing with him had, in fact, kept her mind off the cold, the storm, and the dragon raging outside— but also that he had provoked her specifically for that reason.

Which, she hated to admit, was exactly what her father had done many times: M&M's beside the trail to help a five-year-old Cat forget how tired she was. Songs to detour her tears over a cut finger. Jokes to make her laugh at a less-than-perfect spelling test.

Jonathan Taylor had been a master at distraction when it was most needed.

And now her cousin was doing the same thing.

For the first time since Ty had barged into her life, Cat looked, really looked, into his eyes. What she saw there held no malice, no edge, not even any deception. Just warmth. And despite everything her brain was saying—remember, he's crazy, and a thief—she let her guard down. Because the truth was, to be perfectly honest, she wanted very much to be distracted from the cruel, freezing reality of the moment.

"Okay," she said, "I'll bet you."

Ty clapped his hands. "Cool! Okay, so here are the rules: If Mugs goes for the pizza, then I have to eat a slice. But if he goes for the burrito first, then you have to eat one. Deal?" He stuck his hand out to shake on it.

Cat took it and gave it a yank, then squeezed extra hard to emphasize the point. The bet was on.

It took some doing to get Mugs to back off long enough to set the food out. Ultimately, Cat had to hold him while Ty, under careful observation, set a slice of pizza and one burrito side by side, *exactly* the same distance from Mugs's quivering nose. Finally Ty nodded and said, "Ready, set, go!"

Cat released Mugs, and the food-crazed hound lunged.

CHAPTER 22

PEE-UW!

The burrito vanished in seconds.

"Mugs!" Cat cried. "You traitor!"

Mugs licked his lips and seemed to smile.

Ty couldn't contain his delight. "Ha! I won!"

Cat shot him eye daggers. The wind gusted again, flinging snow into the cave. Cat flinched at the frigid blast.

Ty, on the other hand, acted as if the weather was balmy and there was no emergency. "But, hey, look on the bright side," he said with a grin. "You're a winner, too. Now you get to eat the best food in the whole wide world!" He pulled another burrito from the paper bag and shoved it at her. "Here! *Bon appétit!*"

Cat's glare deepened, but she took the burrito. If nothing else, she was a woman of her word. She pinched her nostrils shut with a thumb and index finger—just to let Ty know how nauseating she found this—and ate the entire thing.

"That's terrible!" she said after the last bite, even though it wasn't true. To her surprise the cold burrito tasted great. Still, she had to maintain appearances. To emphasize her point, she took a big swig of water and rinsed her mouth thoroughly. Then—just to make doubly sure Ty got the point—she turned her head and spat hard out of the snow cave's opening.

Mugs's head shot up, and he charged out into the storm as if Cat had spit a burrito for him to fetch. Ty found this insanely funny, especially when Mugs came racing back in, coated with snow. "Too wild and woolly out there, huh, Mugs!" he hooted.

Cat laughed, too, grateful for the amusement. Grateful, too, for Ty. Although she'd never admit it out loud, at that moment she was glad he had bulldozed his way back into her life.

Until a smell like rotten eggs scorched her nostrils. "Yuck!" Cat said. "See why I don't eat bean burritos?"

"What?" Ty said. "I didn't fart. It was you!"

"No way!" Cat scowled. "I only ate one burrito. You ate, like, a dozen." She waved her hands to try to clear the air. "You're the guilty one!"

Ty elbowed Cat hard. "Am not! It was you, who—"

Another wave of noxious gas filled the snow cave.

Reality hit them both at the same moment.

"Mugs!" they howled. "Bad dog!"

Mugs cowered, then squirmed close and nuzzled Cat's hand as if to apologize. Cat relented and hugged the stinky pooch tight.

"Wow!" she said. "Mugs is really warm, like a heater."

Ty laid his hand on Mugs's chest. His eyes lit up. "Hey, what if . . ."

Cat was already one step ahead of him, searching through a side pocket in her backpack. She found what she was looking for—an emergency blanket. Why hadn't she thought of that before? With its reflective Mylar™ coating and Mugs-the-smelly-heater, maybe they could get a little warmer, push away the dangerous shivering signs of hypothermia.

Cat unfolded the emergency blanket and laid it over Ty and herself, then pulled Mugs in between them. Slowly the temperature started to rise.

So did more smelly air.

Cat and Ty both let out loud groans and pinched their nostrils shut.

"Aw, Mugs, that's awful!" Ty moaned. "Forget the storm killing us, you will!" He faked his last gasping breaths and clutched his throat. "I . . . can't . . . breathe!"

Cat grinned. "What a way to go."

As if on cue, another wave of stench rose from under the emergency blanket.

"Pee-uw!" Ty and Cat both sang, "Dog farts! Dog farts! Dog farts!" as outside the dragon raged across Storm Mountain.

CHAPTER 23

DRAGON FANGS

Cat wasn't sure when she dozed off. Ty had kept her entertained in his hyper way for what seemed like hours: doing impressions of Elvis one minute, then insisting they play Name That Tune the next, and then solitaire with imaginary cards. All of this while leading "warm-up" calisthenics with their fingers and toes. The last thing she remembered was him softly singing "She'll Be Comin' Round the Mountain" in hip-hop style, with a country twang. Now she woke to pitch black and snow stinging her face.

Disoriented, stiff with cold, Cat fumbled around in the top pouch of her backpack and found her headlamp. When she finally got it in place over her hood and clicked it on, she came instantly and completely awake. Snow was blowing directly in on them. A fine dust of white whirled before her eyes. Already the emergency blanket was coated with a thin layer, and it was building up fast.

Cat's headlamp beam fell on the snow cave's entrance. It was twice the size it had been when she and Ty and Mugs had first crawled in. It had partially fallen in and was now funneling the storm directly at them. If the cave collapsed any more, they'd be completely exposed. Exposure in a storm like this meant certain death. Was this what had happened to Dad and Uncle Scott? Had they wakened in the night to find the only protection they had was being torn from around them?

Cat tried to push the possibility from her mind. Maybe if she just ignored it, it would go away. They still had their little doggy heater doing his job. She could hear Mugs's noisy breathing beneath the blanket. Ty's, too. The fog of his breath plumed into the icy air. Maybe she could just wait out the blizzard. Or at least wait out the wind. It shifted once. It could shift again. Maybe even calm down.

It did neither. A great blast kicked up snow and flung it in Cat's face. She recoiled as it slapped. The wind howled. A piece of the snow cave's roof fell on Cat's feet. There would be no reprieve.

Cat sat up and crawled out from under the emergency blanket. Immediately, she was hit by the cold. Its icy fingers wrapped around her neck and pried at her collar. She cinched her hood tighter. The sooner she got this fixed, the sooner she could get back under the blanket and soak up the relative warmth there.

It took a minute to find her shovel, buried under spindrift. Once in hand, she set to work flinging the quickly accumulating snow out into the night.

It flew back in at her in a frozen spray.

A hollow formed in the pit of Cat's stomach. She fought it

with logic and reason. *Think! Focus!* Wind was the problem. You couldn't stop the wind. But you could block it. Only question was how.

She remembered reading a *National Geographic* article about how Inuits in the far north built igloos. Maybe she could cut a block of wind-packed snow and wedge it into the hole, make a door.

Using her shovel as a knife, Cat dug a lunch tray–size chunk from the inside of the snow cave's floor and gently lifted it. Awkward as it was, she still managed to lean it carefully into place.

The difference was immediate, as the new "door" shut out much of the gale. But tendrils of cold still crept in around the edges, and a big hole remained at the top.

Cat chipped off another chunk of snow to fill the gap. She wedged it in place, then began stuffing loose snow in around the remaining cracks. Just a bit more and they'd be in protected space again. She gave it one final pat, and all of her work suddenly crumbled and fell, opening up another, and bigger, hole.

The wind screamed as frigid air streamed in on her. Getting more desperate by the moment, Cat grabbed her pack and shoved it into the new hole to block it. For a moment it looked like this was going to do the trick. She sat back and was just about to breathe a sigh of relief when the wind surged into a jet-engine roar and the wall collapsed even more.

The fist of panic gripped her now. She shoved the pack back in place. It fell out again. She turned it, searching desperately for any way to make it work. The top pouch flopped open, and from the main compartment rolled the brass urn, out into the tempest.

"Dad!" Cat lunged through the snow cave's opening after her father's ashes. The storm instantly enveloped her, beat at her with furious freezing fists. She groped blindly for the urn. The side of her hand thumped it, and it slid farther away. "No!" She searched frantically. An explosion of wind knocked her flat. Her headlamp flew from her head, its beam shining straight up into the knifing snow.

Cat stumbled over to it and swept the beam across the ground. There! A small glint of brass. She lurched over to the urn. It was already half buried. She scooped snow away and clutched it to her.

The storm ramped up even more, exploding out of the darkness. Cat shivered, disoriented. She had to get back into the cave. Even if it was falling apart, it was better than being completely out in the open.

But where was it? She couldn't see two feet. For a few moments she floundered randomly about. Until she kicked something with her foot—her pack, still in the snow cave's entrance. She ducked down and into what was left of the shelter.

It was only when she had slumped onto her side that she realized that she was actually holding her dad's urn—for the first time, ever.

At first she felt nothing but shock. The urn was so small—no bigger than a football, really. And weighed so little. It couldn't be much more than eight pounds, maybe ten at most? How could a man that had lived so large a life—the great mountaineer Jonathan Taylor, who'd summited peaks all over the world, rescued stranded climbers, and even donated one of his kidneys to his twin brother—how could he be reduced to such compact lightness?

And yet . . .

And yet somehow the urn carried the weight of so many memories:

Cat and her dad sitting on the couch together, reading *Where the Wild Things Are* for the umpteenth time.

The feel of Dad's unshaven face first thing in the morning. Cat had called it "Daddy's cactus."

The smell of wood smoke in Dad's shirt.

The dark hair on the back of Dad's hands.

The sound of Dad's voice, deep and powerful but also gentle and kind.

The goofiness—Dad pointing a flashlight in one ear and asking Cat if she could see light coming out the other side. "If you do," he had said, laughing, "I qualify for mountain rescue work!"

Yes, Dad had loved to laugh, and play, especially with his only daughter. When Cat was little, their favorite game was tiger. Dad would go into the hall and wait while Cat hid behind the couch. Then Dad would get down on all fours and come tiger-prowling into the living room. He would growl. Cat would giggle, then pounce on the tiger's back. They would roll around on the carpet,

Dad roaring and lashing with imaginary claws. But ultimately, he'd give up and cry *uncle*!

Uncle. That's right, Uncle Scott had loved to play tiger, too, as had Ty. Her cousin would fling himself at the tigers with wild abandon, his joyous peals of laughter ringing through the house. Eventually, Mom and Aunt Lizzy would be drawn into the room and join the bedlam. Soon all six of the Taylors would be rolling and wrestling and laughing on the living room floor, one big happy family.

Hot tears welled up in Cat's eyes. She wiped at them, but it was no use. They spilled over onto her cheeks and onto the urn, where they froze as they ran down its sides.

The wind screamed, slamming its fist into the cave. The emergency blanket cracked like a whip. Needles of snow slashed at Cat's cheeks. Another section of the cave collapsed. It was being torn apart. It was only a matter of time.

"No," Cat said, and with that single word came a sudden calm. And the assurance—not logical, but from deep down in her gut—that there was only one thing to do, what Dad would do.

Hugging the urn close, Cat turned and blocked the storm with her body. The blizzard rose to hammer force, pummeling Cat's back, howling her name. She shivered as its freezing fangs pierced deep. She curled into a ball, her father's ashes at her core, and closed her eyes. The cold gave way to numbness, both of body and of mind. Cat relented and gave herself up to the dragon.

CHAPTER 24

A CHIP OFF THE OLD BLOCK

At first the voice seemed to be coming from one direction and then from another, like an echo ricocheting off canyon walls. From deep in her being, Cat struggled to distinguish individual words, but they were jumbled and any message lost.

Still, there was something about the voice, despite her disorientation, that sounded vaguely familiar. It faded for a moment, and Cat felt herself sinking back into the listless haze that weighted her down. Falling . . . falling . . .

Was this death? Everything seemed so surreal, distant, dreamlike.

Cat's eyelids felt like they were made of cold stone, but she worked hard and finally opened them into tiny slits. All she saw was a bright whiteness shimmering in her narrow field of vision. She thought of brushing it away, and even willed her hand to do it, but found she couldn't move.

In the distance, as if from another dimension, the voice came again. It was directional now, but still nothing more than a garble of sound. Human?

It faded. Or was it Cat's ability to concentrate? Her body felt lifeless, her brain in a stupor.

This time when Cat heard the voice she knew that, yes, it was human. And familiar.

"Dad?"

Cat wasn't sure if she'd said the word or just thought it. Either way, the concept was startling, and roused her. She fought to climb her way up out of the numbness. Now she actually moved one hand, bringing it to her side. With wooden fingers she touched her jacket. It was stiff and coated with ice.

Slowly, painfully, Cat worked her elbow under her body. The motion brought a dull throb to her knee. She winced, sucking in her breath, but somehow intuitively knew not to stop, not to give in to gravity, lethargy, not to slump back down into the frigid tomb.

The voice came yet again, but more faintly, as if moving away from her. "No, wait," Cat whispered.

She mustered all of her will and pushed up with her elbow. Chunks of snow fell down on her, threatening burial. Adrenaline surged. Cat rammed her fist upward, and suddenly it broke through. Daylight and fresh air spilled in, along with a glimpse of brilliant, clear blue sky.

Cat knocked more snow away until the hole in the roof was larger. With great effort she forced herself up onto her knees, to find herself facing downhill. The boulders of the Hallelujah Gate leaned against one another less than a hundred feet from where she stood, and beyond them the tree line. She'd been so close and hadn't even known.

From behind her Cat heard a call. She twisted around to see a man in a red Storm Mountain Search and Rescue parka climbing up the mountain toward the North Face Direct. All around him the snow field shone brilliant and white, more like an angel's wings than a dragon's. Above it all gleamed the summit of Storm Mountain, high and rugged and . . . magnificent. Her father's mountain.

"Dad?" The word came out nothing more than a hoarse croak.

The man kept climbing, every moment getting farther away.

Cat took a deep breath. Her throat felt as if it were ripping, but the word made it out full force this time. "Dad!"

The man turned. "Cat?"

"*Dad!*" Cat reached out for him, but her head went light. She buckled and collapsed on the snow, calling, "Please. Please. Don't leave me."

The next thing Cat knew, the voice hovered very close, inches from her ear. "Cat?"

She opened her eyes and looked up. For a moment it was her father who knelt there beside her, gently patting her on the shoulder.

But then the man spoke again. "My name is Gary Winter. I'm with Storm Mountain Search and Rescue. I was a friend of your father's. I'm here to help."

As he talked, he was opening his pack and pulling out a sleeping bag. He laid it across her. "The sheriff's department was able to trace the general location of your nine-one-one call before the signal went dead," he said. "But when the storm roared in, we got shut down. We were afraid this was going to turn from a rescue into a recovery. I'm so glad you did the right thing and dug in. Nine-one-one couldn't make out everything you said—your call was breaking up—but we got the impression there was someone else up here with—"

A cry of anguish from under the snow cut Gary Winter short. "Get me out of here! Mugs farted again!"

Gary's look of surprise quickly melted into a grin. "Sounds like an emergency," he said with a wink.

He started pulling snow away, digging toward Ty and Mugs. Cat sat up to help, but then realized that she still clutched her father's urn to her with one numb arm.

"It's okay," Gary said. He glanced at the urn. "You've had a rough night. Just sit tight and let me do the work."

Cat shook her head. "I want to help."

Gary looked her in the eye and nodded. "Just like your dad," he said with a smile, "a chip off the old block."

Cat tried to smile back, but her mouth wouldn't respond properly. Her cheeks were too numb. "Thanks," she said, and together she and Gary Winter made the rescue.

CHAPTER 25

ASHES TO ASHES

What Cat imagined as the resolution to her epic on Storm Mountain included an escort home, the return of her father's ashes to their rightful place on the mantel, a hot bath, fresh-baked pesto pizza with a mocha chaser, and the rest of the day on the couch in front of the TV, napping. Mom would return that evening and never know the difference.

What she got instead was dizzy, then faint, followed by fleeting, disjointed bits of consciousness:

Gary Winter radioing for assistance.

A small army of Storm Mountain Search and Rescue members gathered around with concerned looks on their faces.

Something about Ty's toes and frostbite.

Bits of a discussion about getting Mugs to a vet.

The *thwock-thwock-thwock* of helicopter rotors, then the big bird lifting off the snow as a woman with kind eyes administered an IV.

She came to again for a brief moment in the Good Samaritan Hospital emergency room amidst lots of voices. For a moment a physician's face appeared out of the blur. "Hi, I'm Dr. Wilson," he said, then faded. The next time she woke, she found herself in the intensive care unit, and looked over to see her mother sitting beside her bed, face streaked with tears.

Later Cat would find out that unanswered calls to Hope's cell phone had first alerted her mom that something was wrong. Then the voice mail from Aunt Lizzy saying that Ty was missing, along with Uncle Scott's climbing gear and his ashes. She wanted to know if Ty had shown up at their house. Not more than two minutes later Hope had gotten a call from the Storm County Sheriff's Department. She was out of the software developers' conference and running for her car within seconds.

Now, though, Hope couldn't speak, only wrap her arms around her daughter. Tears sprang to Cat's eyes, and she hugged her mom back. It wasn't until she looked over Hope's shoulder that she saw the camera lens in the doorway pointed straight at them. A reporter had snuck onto the floor with a videographer and captured the moment. A worried mother's tearful reunion with her daughter became headline footage on the evening news.

"Su-weet!" Ty said, when he hobbled in the next morning. "You've gone nationwide, all networks plus cable!"

He only had frostnip on his toes, not frostbite, he informed them, no permanent damage. And his head was still screwed on straight. Well, sort of.

But who cared. There were more cameras and reporters outside in the hospital parking lot than you could shake a stick at, and they wanted to interview Cat, and him, too! "What do you say, Cuz? This is our big chance!"

With moms at their sides—Aunt Lizzy had shown up around midnight—Cat and Ty ventured out into a sea of TV vans.

A shout went up. "There they are!" Reporters came running. In seconds they were engulfed in a media frenzy.

"Tell our audience, how you are feeling?" one reporter said, turning Ty toward a camera.

"This is Cat Taylor, daughter of the mountaineering great, Jonathan Taylor," another announced as she shoved a mic in Cat's face, "who died on this same cruel, unforgiving peak . . ."

All became a blur of questions, broken only when Gary Winter of Storm Mountain Search and Rescue walked through the crowd leading an exuberant husky on a practice-rope leash.

"Mugs!" Cat and Ty both shouted, and that reunion was broadcast live across the nation, too.

"We're famous!" Ty exclaimed later. "Like rock stars!"

And they were, for a day, anyway. But with a happy ending recorded, the cameras and reporters quickly moved on to other stories. Cat and Ty were released from the hospital, sent off with hugs from their nurses and handshakes from the docs. Without much more than a "We'll talk," Ty and Aunt Lizzy left for Seattle. Cat and Hope drove up Storm Mountain Road in silence.

Until they got into the house and the hammer came down.

"You could have been killed! What were you thinking?" Hope demanded.

Cat was tempted to blame Ty—he had, in fact, started the whole crazy mess—but found herself, for some reason she couldn't explain, unwilling to rat on her cousin. She just shrugged and said, "I don't know."

She was grounded for two weeks, but Ty e-mailed that Aunt Lizzy had had a hissy fit all the way home and grounded him for a month. So at least there was some justice in the world.

Cat rubbed it in with a text message.

Ty rubbed right back, and then followed up with a series of good-natured insults via Cat's Facebook page. Soon the two were joking around like old times and arguing over the best food in the world.

Memorial Day brought a new twist. Ty relayed that "in a moment of maternal weakness," his mom had actually been able to discuss Ty's desire to spread his father's ashes. "Get this!" he wrote. "Mom says that if it will make me feel better, then why not, let's do it."

Aunt Lizzy called Hope to confirm, encouraging Hope to spread Jonathan's ashes, too. "Put it all to rest."

Cat texted Ty while her mom and Aunt Lizzy were still on the phone. "No way will Hope Taylor go for that," she wrote. "You two are wasting your time."

"Wanna bet?" Ty texted back. Turned out he knew something about Hope that Cat didn't. She had confided to Aunt Lizzy that she'd gone to the software developers' conference in Portland for a reason beyond giving a presentation. She had shared the podium with another freelancer, named Richard . . .

"Do you mean to tell me you faced your biggest fear of speaking in public to be with a guy?" Cat asked her mom as soon as she hung up. "Why didn't you tell me?"

"Do you tell me everything?" Hope said.

Cat answered with a practiced glare.

"I thought as much," Hope said. "Well, it's the same for me. There are some things a mother just doesn't want to discuss with her daughter, at least not until the time is right."

Cat could only stare, trying to wrap her head—and her heart—around the idea. She knew she should be happy for her mom. Still, this was going to take some getting used to.

"I don't know what will come of this relationship," Hope continued. "But I do know it's finally time to move on. I've been considering Ty's idea, and, well, I think it might be a good one." She then broke into a sudden smile, as if a great weight had been lifted from her shoulders.

"Wait a minute," Cat said. "Are you saying that you actually want to spread Dad's ashes, too?"

Hope nodded. She could only part with a portion of them for starters. But, yes, she thought spreading a bit of Jonathan's remains would be a step toward healing.

All of which sounded . . . fine, Cat guessed, until Hope

explained that this "step toward healing" wasn't to be sprinkling a few of Dad's ashes in with the root-ball of a newly planted apple tree in the backyard, or letting some wash down Cascade Creek and eventually out to sea. The plan that Ty insisted on, and that both mothers had evidently embraced, was to spread them from the summit of Storm Mountain.

True, they wouldn't attempt the North Face Direct. Instead, they'd climb the west side of the peak on the easiest route possible—the Dog Walk Ridge.

Still, it was Storm Mountain. What if the dragon woke again?

CHAPTER 26

IN MEMORIUM

They drove to the trailhead in the predawn darkness of June 23. Hope and Aunt Lizzy had picked that particular date because it was the birthday of the twins, Jonathan and Scott Taylor.

"It would be fitting, don't you think," Hope had said, "to celebrate their lives on the anniversary of their births?"

Cat had nodded. "Sure, Mom." Although once they parked and she clambered out of the car into the crisp morning air, and saw the great triangular silhouette of Storm Mountain looming above them in the dark, she suddenly wasn't sure at all. She dropped her gaze and busied herself with getting her headlamp on and tying double knots in her climbing-boot laces.

Ty was already prancing around like a horse in the starting gate. "C'mon!" he urged. "Let's get this show on the road! Right, Mugsy?"

Mugs wagged his tail and barked his delight. He was there at

Ty's insistence. "How could we not take a dog on a route called the Dog Walk?"

Cat agreed. Mugs deserved to go. Hope and Lizzy had given in without much of a fight.

Still, Cat had imagined the climb to spread her father's ashes as being a somber event, not necessarily funereal, but at least thoughtful, respectful of the departed. Now it seemed to be turning into . . . something else. Part Comedy Central. Part circus. Part reality TV. As if to keep up with Ty, the mothers were putting on quite a show of being upbeat.

"Just like old times!" Aunt Lizzy said to Hope as she shouldered her pack. "Remember that first double date with the Taylor twins? It was this very climb!"

Hope nodded and smiled. "They were testing us, really, to see if we had what it took to be their girlfriends."

"We did!" Aunt Lizzy exclaimed. "If I remember correctly, we even beat them to the top."

"Yep," Hope agreed. "Caught them off guard when we surged up the last hundred feet. They didn't know we were both training for the Portland Marathon. Ha!"

Cat smiled at the banter, glad to see her mom enjoying herself. She shouldered her pack and wondered if she'd loaded in too much gear. It seemed heavier than last night when she was packing, and repacking, and repacking again.

"Okay, let's hit the trail," Aunt Lizzy said.

"Yee-haw!" Ty hooted. He bolted to the head of the line, chatting, even singing, hamming up an imitation of Julie Andrews in

The Sound of Music. "The hills are aliiiiiiiive, with the sound of mew-zick!"

The sky began to gradually lighten as they walked through the waking forest. Pink and orange highlights blended with robin's-egg blue. Headlamps clicked off and went back into packs. Birds began to stir, singing up the sun.

The golden orb cracked the horizon just as they emerged from the trees, illuminating Dog Walk Ridge. Cat could see that the recent run of hot weather had pushed the snow line up to over 7,500 feet, revealing alpine meadows awash in fresh green. Soon the landscape steepened, and they were pushing through dew-soaked grasses. Purple lupine blooms were opening up for the day, as were the deep red flowers of Indian paintbrush.

Open space kicked Mugs into an even higher gear. He ran ahead, chasing after ground squirrels, then fat marmots that whistled to alert all the wildlife of the alpine scourge.

"That dog is going to log twenty times the mileage we do," cracked Aunt Lizzy.

Hope laughed. Cat just nodded. Although hardly sleeping the night before, now that they were actually climbing, she felt a sense of calm, and purpose, and, most surprisingly, confidence. Dad was with her, at least in part. A Ziploc bag in her pocket held ten tablespoons of his ashes. She'd cried herself to sleep two weeks in a row, but now felt better. Somehow stronger, too. She felt her father's presence. She could do this thing.

They reached the snow line just below Bowsprit Rock by eight A.M., as planned, and stopped to strap on crampons and slip ice ax leashes over their wrists. At Hope's insistence, everyone took a nibble of her dried apricots and drank some water. Also at Hope's insistence, they roped up, tying in with figure-eight follow-throughs on the front (Lizzy) and back (Hope), and butterfly knots to secure Ty and Cat in the middle. Cat leashed Mugs to her climbing harness with her practice rope, tying the figure-eight follow-through and locking it off with a stopper knot.

The angle of the sun steepened, as did the angle of the slope. Dog Walk Ridge narrowed as they skirted the eroded crater. Cat could smell sulfur, evidence that although this old volcano wasn't active, it wasn't extinct, either. Dragon's breath.

She pushed the thought from her mind and concentrated on each step. She was breathing hard. Which surprised her. She'd trained for this, trail running every day after school and on weekends. But her pack felt heavier by the moment, and her legs, too.

Pressure breathing, or mountain breath—like she'd done on the North Side in May—seemed the logical solution. Step, breath, rest. Step, breath, rest. It helped, but still the summit looked so far away. She kept her head down and tried not to think about how long it would take, or the one crevasse at the top of the Luebben Glacier. Called a bergschrund, they would have to detour around it to reach the final pitch to the summit.

Ty had no such issues. He stopped and looked down into the blue-tinted abyss with a grin. "Hey, Cat, how about we drop in and say hello to the ice fairies? You know, just for old times sake?"

Cat rolled her eyes and tried to look nonchalant. "Yeah, right," she said. "While we're at it, we could set up a haul system and actually pull you out this time, too."

After Ty had moved on, Hope asked quietly from behind, "You okay? We don't have to do this, you know."

Cat reached into her pocket and gripped the bag of ashes. "Yes, we do," she said.

Conversation dwindled, even from Ty. They were approaching 11,000 feet of elevation by now. Thin air slowed the pace. Each step required thought and effort.

But just when Cat found herself thinking that the climb might really go on forever, the slope eased and she looked up to see that there was no more up to ascend. She stood on the summit of Storm Mountain.

"Whoa!" Ty shouted. "How cool is this?"

Cat turned in a slow circle, taking in the panorama. To the north jutted Mount Adams and Mount Saint Helens, and beyond them the massive bulk of Mount Rainier. To the west spread the Willamette Valley and distant coast range. Lined up to the south stood Mount Jefferson and the Three Sisters. In the east, across the high desert, Cat was sure she could detect the curvature of the earth. Very cool, indeed.

They sat in a circle for the memorial. Each person said a few words, mostly funny stories. Cat told of the time her father accidentally squirted ketchup on his head. Ty recounted that Halloween when his dad absentmindedly ate every single piece of Ty's candy, then had to run to the store to replace it all. Hope remembered the day Jonathan cut his finger, then, to his great embarrassment, fainted. Aunt Lizzy sang her and Scott's favorite Beatle's tune—"I Wanna Hold Your Hand."

When everyone had had a say, Cat pulled the zippered bag of her father's ashes from her pocket. Out of Ty's pack emerged a plastic container of Scott Taylor's.

Cat held her dad's ashes out to her mother. "Here," she said, "you do it."

Hope shook her head. "No, we'll do it together."

They stood and each held a corner of the baggy, then opened it and flung the ashes into the wind. Like a puff of smoke, the ashes drifted from the summit, out over the North Face Direct and the Hood Glacier far below.

Cat looked over to see tears trailing down her mother's face. Hope wiped at them and forced a smile. Cat smiled back, her eyes brimming, too.

Afterward, they ate bean burritos and homemade pesto pizza. Mugs had to settle for a Milk Bone dog treat. In the name of peace and solidarity, Cat took a bite of burrito without making a face or spitting. Ty scarfed as much pizza as he could get his hands on until Cat slapped the back of his wrist and shook a finger at him.

"This is good," Ty said, "but wouldn't it all taste even better washed down with a double-shot mocha? Or, better yet, big swigs of Mountain Dew?"

Cat shook her head. "You just can't let it go, can you?" she teased. "Anyway, who would be stupid enough to carry all of that heavy stuff up here?"

"You would," Ty said, as if it were a matter of fact.

Cat scowled. "I would not!"

"Would to."

"Would not!"

A mischievous smile crept onto Ty's face. He pointed to Cat's pack. "What's that I see poking out there against the cloth? Sure looks like a can to me. . . ."

Cat looked at where Ty was pointing. Sure enough, the outline of a can showed clearly against the nylon.

"*What?*" She yanked the pack open, then dug down to the bottom. Her hand came upon a can, then another. "You've got to be kidding me!" She turned the pack upside down and dumped its contents out onto the summit. Four bottles of Starbucks Mocha spilled out onto the snow, and four cans of Mountain Dew. "How did this get—" Then it hit her. "Ty!"

He was already doubled over with laughter. "Woo-hoo!" he yelled. "I snuck it all in there this morning when you were still asleep. Ha! Gotcha!"

Cat glared. "Very funny," she said, and began shaking one of the Mountain Dews.

Ty's eyes went wide. "No! Don't—"

Cat just laughed and popped the top. An arc of Mountain Dew erupted volcano-like out of the can in a perfect, deadly arc, catching Ty in the shoulder. He yelped and grabbed a can, gave it three quick shakes, and aimed it at Cat. Hope and Aunt Lizzy quickly scooped up ammunition. Mugs barked in delight. Within seconds the war was on.